break away

BREAKAWAY

A Nashville Knights Novel

EMILY SILVER

*To those finding their place in life
Don't be afraid to start over. You can discover something new wherever
you are in life.*

I know I did <3

Chapter One

CHLOE

I don't think I can do this. Oh God, why did I think I could do this? I mean, when Duncan got down on one knee, the only thing I could have said was yes. It would've been rude to say no.

Smoothing a hand down the front of my white dress—my *too* white dress—it hits me that I can't do this. It's not my style. The mermaid skirt is too tight around my legs. There's too much lace on the bodice. The rhinestones? The saleswoman and my mother talked me into them.

And why is it so damn itchy?

They said how good the rhinestones would look as I walked down the aisle toward Duncan.

Duncan.

My fiancé.

The man I'm going to marry.

The thought of that has bile rising in my throat.

I can't. God, I really can't do this.

Maybe I could talk to Duncan and get a read on him before I walk down the aisle. That's a perfectly normal thing to do, right?

He wanted to keep the wedding traditional. Not spend the night before together. Not see one another. No first look before the ceremony.

I went along with all of it.

Until now.

Hiking up my dress and kicking off my heels, I dash out of my room. Thank God I kicked everyone out earlier to take a few minutes to myself.

Walking down the beige halls, I follow the signs to the Fletcher Wedding Party. I hear Duncan's voice as I pad my way down the hall. Other than his voice, it's quiet.

"Baby, it's going to be okay."

Baby? What the hell? Who is he talking to? It stops me in my tracks.

"Look, I told you all of this last night."

Is *this* why he didn't want to spend the night together?

I slink farther along the hall, finding the door that's cracked open.

"You have to be patient. I promise. Once things settle down after the honeymoon, we can see each other."

After the honeymoon?

"That's right. I love you."

I love you?

Okay, what the fuck is going on?

I'm ready to burst in there and yell at the man I'm supposed to be marrying in less than thirty minutes, but his next comment stops me.

"Do you really think I'd marry someone so boring? I mean, c'mon. Chloe is not the right person for me."

I can't hear whoever is on the other line, but me? Boring? I thought Duncan and I had fun together. I mean, sure, I like my Saturday mornings at the farmers' market, and wine nights with my girls, but does that make me boring?

"That's right, baby. Only you. I love *you*. Once I get back into the league, I'll be free and clear. Having a Goody Two-shoes like Chloe? It'll help improve my image. Show them that I'm a changed man so a team will finally pick me up again."

A changed man? Free and clear? From *me*?

Anger boils in my veins. Are. You. Fucking. Kidding. Me?

The man on the other side of this door is telling another woman that *he* loves *her*. The same man who told *me* he loved me yesterday before I left for the hotel and packed my bag for the honeymoon.

Not wanting to give away my position, I tiptoe back the way I came. My vision blurs as tears of rage gather in my eyes.

I'm boring? If I'm so boring, why would Duncan propose to me? We'd only been back together for a few months before he proposed, and I've spent the better part of the last eight or so months planning the wedding. Fast? Maybe, but people fall in love and get married way faster than that.

Was it *too* fast? Was it only so he could get picked up by a team again? Is that why there's another woman?

I cannot believe I let myself get suckered in by this man.

Duncan Fletcher. The man I thought I was in love with is actually the biggest douche nozzle on the planet.

Bursting back into my room, I slam the door shut behind me and find my bag. I pull out my phone and start typing away a message to the Fletcher that will never let me down.

CHLOE

I need you

HIS RESPONSE IS IMMEDIATE.

DAX

Is everything okay?

No

Bring your car keys

Fuck. What happened?

Just get here now

"CHLOE? Honey? We need to get going if the ceremony is going to start on time," Mom's voice rings through the door.

"I need a few more minutes," I call back.

"Chloe, we can't keep everyone waiting."

"They're not going to start without me!" I snap.

There's muttering on the other side of the door. Honestly, I don't care at this point. Whatever I was feeling before is nothing compared to now as I pace in front of the mirror. I catch sight of my dress and it turns the anger into fury.

How could I let myself get this far?

Grabbing the hem of the dress, I rip it. Hard. God, I hate this frock, and the sound of shredding fabric fills my ears. I keep ripping until every scrap of fabric is off my body. I breathe a sigh of relief as the material falls away.

Piles of organza silk and satin lie in ruined piles on the floor as I stand in my corset.

"You think I'm boring now, Duncan?" I kick the material out of the way, running to the closet to grab my jacket and sweatpants.

If I'm going to get out of here, I need to at least be wearing something.

"Chloe? Are you okay?"

A knock followed by Dax's voice calms me. Even for a moment.

Rushing to the door, I pull it open and usher him inside. "Get in here."

His hand is over his eyes. "Am I allowed to see you?"

"Yes. Besides, it doesn't matter."

I yank his hand down, and when he looks at me, I can see the confusion wash over his face.

He points at what I'm wearing. "Why aren't you wearing your dress?"

I throw a thumb over my shoulder. "It's over there. But that's not why I need you."

"Chloe, what is going on?" he asks. "Why do you need me? And why did I need my car keys?"

"Because we're getting out of here."

"Out of here? You're getting married in like ten minutes."

"Not anymore." I brush past him and grab my purse. "Are you going to help me or what?"

"Obviously. But are you not going to tell me what's going on?"

I shake my head. "Not right now. We need to get out of here before anyone comes looking for me."

"You're the bride," Dax points out. "You realize people

will come looking, right? I mean, your mom and bridesmaids are waiting for you."

"Ugh." I throw my head back in frustration. "Look, if you don't want to help, I can call a rideshare."

"No." Dax pulls his keys out of his pocket. "Do you need anything from me?"

I look behind me at the side exit door. "Will you just tell my parents and then I'll meet you at your car? Please, Dax?"

A pinched look washes over his face. "You really want me to tell your parents that the wedding is off?"

"Yes. If I try to do it, my mom will talk me back into it and I do *not* want that."

"Fine." Dax waves me toward the door. "Go. I'll take care of everyone else, okay?"

I press up onto my toes and peck his cheek. "Thank you."

Getting to the side door, I grab my bag I had stuffed with essentials from the last few days and turn back as Dax takes a deep breath and leaves. At least I have him in my corner.

Because it's a gorgeous day here, everyone is filling the park. It gives me the cover I need to dodge through people to get to the parking lot. Clicking the fob on Dax's keys, I follow the beeping until I find his small, black SUV and hop into the front seat.

Flipping the visor down, I start to pull the bobby pins out of my blonde hair. It's tucked, twisted, and sprayed to within an inch of its life.

Something else I didn't like. A fancy French twist that my stylist said would complement my dress. I said yes because I didn't want to hurt her feelings.

Tears start to burn again. This time, hurt seeps through the anger. How did I let it get this far? Instead of standing under a pergola, confessing my love to Duncan, I'm sitting in his brother's car waiting to leave my own wedding.

I blow out a breath, picking at my French manicure. There will be time to figure out what went wrong, but right now, I need copious amounts of alcohol to deal with what I heard.

How could I have gotten played like this?

Dax is running toward me, undoing his purple tie as he crosses the parking lot. His normally curly brown hair is gelled into place. Sunglasses hide his brown eyes as he opens the door and slides inside.

"How did it go?" I wring my hands in my lap as Dax starts the car.

"Well, your mom is likely going to kill me, but other than that, it went about as well as it could. Considering I know absolutely nothing…"

"God, Dax. I'm sorry. I'm so sorry." I throw my head back against the seat as we pull out of the parking lot.

"You know I would do anything for you, Chloe, but you have to tell me what is going on."

I wince, turning my head to look at him. "We need shots for that."

"Okay. Where do you want to go?"

"For now? Drive. Just drive."

Chapter Two

DAX

"**D**oes this place look good?"

Turning into a space in the parking lot of a dive bar, I face Chloe in the front seat. She's picking at the frayed hem of the sweatshirt she's wearing.

"What?"

She glances up, big blue eyes staring back at me. It's hard to pin down the emotions there. Anger. Sadness. Rage.

Considering we were supposed to be at her wedding reception right about now, it doesn't surprise me.

"This bar. Does it work?" A neon sign flashes over a nondescript black door. The sign is the only giveaway that it's a bar. "It was the closest place that I could find that was open."

Chloe unbuckles her seatbelt. "It's fine. As long as they have tequila."

Jumping out the door to follow her inside, I see that the interior matches the exterior. More black walls. Sticky floors. A few pool tables scattered around with a long bar lining the opposite wall.

With only a few patrons lingering around high-top tables, I doubt anyone is going to pay much attention to us in here. Which is exactly what I need to figure out what the fuck happened.

"A bottle of tequila," Chloe tells the bartender as she takes a seat on a wobbly barstool.

"A bottle or a shot?" he questions, running a cloth over a glass.

"Bottle. Two glasses, please," Chloe says.

"You got it." He nods at her and fishes a bottle from the back wall to bring over to us.

I pull my credit card out of my wallet and pass it over to him. "And maybe a couple of waters too."

I have a feeling we're going to be here for a while. Grabbing the empty glasses, I pour us each a drink.

"What are we toasting—" I can't even finish before Chloe is knocking it back.

"More." She snaps her fingers at me.

I do as she asks and she swallows it in one gulp.

But before I pour another, I take her glass and push the water in front of her.

"Okay, at least have a drink of water to chase it. I don't need you turning into a puddle of tequila. And I need you sober to tell me what happened."

She rolls her eyes. "What happened is your brother is a dick."

I roll my eyes right back at her. "I know that. But why specifically today?"

Chloe grabs the bottle and takes a swig right out of it. I cringe. There is no way that can be sanitary.

"Because he's cheating on me!"

"Wait, what? Since when?"

I wish I could say I was surprised, but I'm not. Duncan really is a dick.

"I don't know. He was telling her he loved her and that they'd see each other after the honeymoon and how I'm not the right person for him and he'd never marry someone so, so…*boring*."

"Her who?" Taking the bottle from her, I suck down my own sip. What a fucking asshole my brother is.

Not only was he marrying the woman I've been in love with, but he was—*is*—cheating on her. He never deserved someone so good. Someone he apparently deems *boring*.

"I don't know!" she shrieks. "He was on the phone with her."

"Can I punch him?"

Chloe grabs the bottle from me and takes a drink. "Not before I do. But that would require seeing him. And I don't know if I ever want to see him again in my life. That bastard. I'd run him over with my car if I could."

"I wish I didn't have to see him again," I mutter, taking the bottle from her and letting the alcohol burn on its way down.

Fuck. That is a cheap tequila, almost guaranteeing a headache in the morning. Even from a few shots.

"Did you know he was cheating on me?" Chloe cuts me a scathing glare. "I swear, if you knew…"

"Relax." I rest my hand on her forearm. "I would never have let you marry my brother if I knew. I promise."

She visibly sags, rubbing the heels of her hands against her eyes. "I knew you wouldn't. But God, I can't trust myself now. I mean, how did I let myself get so taken with a man who called me boring?"

"You're not boring."

Her eyes snap to mine, ignoring what I am saying. "Am I boring?"

"I just answered you. You're not boring."

"You answered too quickly. Guess that answers that

question." She grabs the bottle and pours at least two shots' worth in her glass before taking a sip.

"You're not boring," I promise her. "Duncan didn't deserve someone like you."

"Am I just that unlovable?"

"No." My voice is firm so she knows there is no more argument. "Duncan is the one at fault in this situation, not you. He was not the right guy for you."

"Then who is?"

She pierces me with watery blue eyes.

Me.

I'm the one that will show you what you deserve. Shower you with so much love, you won't know what to do with yourself. The one who will never make you question where his loyalties lie.

"You haven't met him yet," I say instead. No point in confessing my feelings to her when she's one shot away from drunk after running out on my brother.

"I'm going to swear off all men."

"All men? Why don't you start with Duncan and see how you feel in a few years?"

"Do you think I could get away with murdering him?" Chloe asks, ignoring me, swigging her drink. "I mean, if it was a jury of all women, I would definitely get away with it."

"As much as you want to"—hell, get in line, Chloe, because I want to murder him too—"you can't. I'd miss you too much if you did."

"Fine. No plotting his murder, but does that mean I get more tequila?"

The bottle is already way lower than it should be in the time we've been here. Pulling out my phone, I see we've been here longer than I realized.

It's then I notice the slew of missed calls and texts. From the guys to Duncan to my parents.

All of them can wait. Chloe is the only person that matters.

"Will you at least eat something if I say yes?"

Chloe grins at me, nodding. "Yes."

"Good." I wave the bartender over. "Anything on the menu we can order to eat?"

"I can do nachos or a hot pretzel with mustard. If you want food, there's a taco stand down the street."

"Pretzel, please," Chloe tells him. "But what kind of mustard?"

He looks confused. "Dijon?"

"No mustard then. But maybe a side of cheese if you have it."

He looks to me as if to confirm what she asked for and I nod. Don't mess with a drunk bride.

"Got it."

"Ugh. It's probably because I like yellow mustard."

Hiccup.

"What are you talking about?"

"Keep up, Dax." Her words start slurring together. Chloe has never been one to hold her alcohol well. Throw in cheap tequila and she's going to be feeling it in the morning. "I get yellow mustard on my ham sandwiches. That's it. Maybe if I was a spicy mustard kind of girl, Duncan wouldn't find me so boring."

"I don't think your mustard preference is the reason he finds you boring."

"But what if I want to be a spicy mustard girl? I could be," she says.

"Can you?"

"No." She buries her face in her hands. "I don't like

spicy mustard. What's wrong with good old-fashioned yellow mustard?"

All I can do is rub comforting circles on her back as the tears finally start.

"There is nothing wrong with yellow mustard. I happen to love yellow mustard."

"You do?" She peeks one eye over at me.

I nod. "Yes. It's my favorite kind."

"You're only saying that to make me feel worse."

"Better, you mean?" I quirk a brow at her, tucking a loose strand of hair behind her ear.

"That's what I said."

A steaming pretzel and a cup of nacho cheese is set in front of us. I nod in thanks and push it closer to Chloe. "You need to eat."

"At least it's nacho cheese."

"I know." Smiling at her, I rip a bite off for myself and dunk it into the metal ramekin. Fuck, that's good. I'm starving.

Because we ran out, we are missing the food at the reception, and before that, I was too anxious to eat.

The last thing I wanted was to watch Chloe marry my brother. My goal was to get drunk enough at the reception to not remember a second of it.

Now? Now I have no idea what is going to happen because Chloe is sitting next to me in a dive bar instead of dancing the night away.

"Maybe I could be nacho cheese. It's spicy enough to not be boring." Another hiccup as she stares into the tiny container of cheese.

"Okay, Chloe. I think it's about time we cut you off." I smile at her. "No more wishing you were food."

Pulling the almost empty bottle away from her, I slide her water glass closer to her.

"Where am I supposed to go tonight? It's not like I can go back to our place."

"How about we go up to my cabin for a few days?"

"Really?" Chloe sways on her stool. "You'd do that for me?"

I clasp a steadying hand over her elbow. "You know I would do anything for you."

"But he's your brother."

"And?"

"I love you, Dax. You're the best friend anyone could have ever asked for."

That's me. The best friend. The one that she's never been in love with.

No, she's been in love with my cheating dickhead of a brother.

"I know. You're my best friend too."

It's not like I can tell her I love her. I mean, I do, but not in the same way she loves me.

Before either of us can say anything else, her head thunks to the bar top.

Fuck.

I wish I could hear her saying those words to me in a different way. But right now, her emotions are a jumbled mess because of leaving Duncan and her wedding behind.

Right now, my best friend needs me more than ever. I'll be there for her no matter how much it hurts.

That's all I can ever be to her.

All because of my fucking dickhead brother.

God, I really do hate him.

Chapter Three

My entire body feels like a lead weight. Mouth? Like sandpaper. My head? It feels like I was clobbered with a sledgehammer.

And then I remember why I feel so crappy.

Duncan is cheating on me and I ran away from my wedding.

I roll over on the soft bed, not caring where my phone is. I have zero doubt there are dozens, if not hundreds, of messages from my family wondering where I am and why I didn't show up. Hell, maybe even Duncan. But wouldn't he just go crying to his girlfriend?

I hate how I'm feeling right now.

Miserable, cranky, and hungover.

The worst combination possible.

I shouldn't put it off. I already did the least adult thing and ran off on Duncan. I need to look and see. And as expected, hundreds of messages. Calls and voicemails from my parents. Texts from Duncan. A few voicemails.

Shit.

This is worse than I thought.

DUNCAN

What the fuck, Chloe?

You ran out on me?

I'm the best thing that ever happened to you and this is how you repay me?

I gave you everything!

Where are you?

Seriously, answer me!

UGH. I don't know what I ever saw in this man. The pressure from my family to settle down made me want to say yes to him. Was there any other reason I said yes? I tap over to the other text from my mom.

MOM

Where in the world are you?

The wedding is supposed to start in ten minutes

Chloe. This behavior is childish

If you don't want to get married, you need to tell someone

Running out on Duncan? He's devastated

DEVASTATED? Really? I highly doubt he was devastated. Probably ran right into the arms of his girlfriend.

Another thought hits me. Oh God. Was *I* the other woman?

Shit. I go back to his texts, ready to fire one off to him.

DUNCAN

Baby. Where are you? I love you

You're the best thing that ever happened to me.

I love you

Call me, okay?

I just want to know you're safe

We can figure this out

"FUCK YOU! Figure it out with your tramp!" I yell, throwing my phone across the room. It clatters to the floor with an unsatisfying clunk. If I felt like getting out of bed, I'd go flush it down the toilet. I never want to speak to him again.

So much for responding like a reasonable adult.

"Seems like someone woke up on the wrong side of the bed."

Sitting up—way too fast for the situation—I feel dizzy and sick when I see Dax, wearing a T-shirt that stretches across his chest and a pair of athletic shorts, standing in the doorframe of the room holding a tray.

"Ugh. Did yesterday really happen?"

"'Fraid so."

"I wish we could rewind it so it never happened."

Dax sets a tray down on the nightstand before walking

to the windows and throwing the curtains open. A steady stream of rain is coming down.

"Then you'd still be getting married to Duncan. Is that what you really want?"

"No." I flop back down on the bed and tug a pillow over my eyes. "I can't believe I almost married someone who is cheating on me."

"At least you ended it before you said I do. That's one bright side."

"I guess you could say that."

"Have you heard from him?"

"Yes."

Dax drops down onto the bed next to me and pulls the tray with two full plates over onto his lap. "And that's why you're throwing things?"

"Yes."

"Maybe eating something will make you feel better."

I sit up, inhaling the scent of bacon, hash browns, eggs, and coffee. "Doubtful, but I won't say no."

Grabbing a piece of crispy bacon from my plate, I bite a piece off.

"Better?" Duncan asks, taking the bottle of ketchup and squeezing it over his hashbrowns.

"Yes." I lean against the bed, munching quietly. "When did you have time to make all of this?"

"Well, when you sleep in, it's easy."

"What time is it?"

"Almost eleven," he tells me.

"Seriously?"

He nods. "I didn't really want to wake you up after yesterday."

"I can't hide forever."

"You can for a few days."

"Really?"

"It's offseason; I have nowhere to be." Dax nods. "You want to try those with mustard?"

I screw my face up in disgust. "Eww, no. Why would I do that?"

"Do you not remember our conversation last night?"

"About mustard? Why would we talk about that?"

"You said maybe if you were spicy mustard, Duncan might like you better."

"I did? Kill me now."

I wish I could drown in my coffee. These last twenty-four hours are not playing out at all how I imagined they would.

I'm not on a plane headed to my honeymoon.

There's no ring on my finger.

I'm not married.

Instead, I'm hungover in my best friend's cabin, debating if eating hash browns will make me want to puke.

Screw it. Might as well try to feel better.

I stab my fork into the fried potato goodness. Okay, this will probably make things a little better.

"Not even using ketchup?" Dax smiles at me.

The fork clatters to the plate as he stretches out across the bed.

"See? I am boring."

"You're not boring," he says, nudging my knee.

"I am. And I need to break out of my shell."

"How are you going to do that?"

Dax leans on one elbow, sipping from his own coffee mug. Black, how he always takes it.

"I'm going to make a to-do list."

"A to-do list to make you less boring? Isn't a list boring to start with?" Dax laughs.

"See if I let you help me with it then."

"What is going to be on this list?"

I take another bite of the hash browns, thinking it over as I chew. "Do you have a pen and paper I can use?"

He hops off the bed and walks over to the desk in the corner. A tiny notebook and pen are thrust into my hands.

"Thanks."

"Does this mean I get to help now?" he asks.

"Maybe." I wink at him.

Flipping open to the first page, I start writing things out. Anything that comes to mind. Things Duncan always shot down whenever I brought them up.

Chloe's Anti-Boring List

Ride a hot-air balloon

Go zip-lining

Try pole dancing

Go skinny-dipping

Run a marathon

Write poetry

Have sex at a sex club with a mustached stranger

Break a world record

Let someone make all my decisions for the day

Try roller derby

Open my own jewelry-making business

I THINK that looks like a good list. I underline a few things to make a point. All things I've wanted to do but never thought I could because I didn't have the courage. Duncan told me they were boring. In other words…they were meant for other, more exciting people.

Not me.

Enough of that.

Any random thing I've ever wanted to do, I'm doing it.

Duncan be damned.

"Are you going to show me?" Dax asks.

"Here." I push it toward him and take a bite of the bacon and eggs. I watch as his eyes read over the list. When he nearly chokes on his coffee, I know exactly where he is.

"This is what's on your list?"

"What's wrong with it?"

"Going to a sex club? You can't do that," Dax hisses.

"Says who?" I set my fork down on my plate and sip on my coffee. So good. Dax knows exactly how I take it—with more creamer than coffee. "Haven't you been to one?"

That earns me a look of shock. "Why would I have gone to one?"

"I don't know. You're more experienced than I am."

"Not in that way." Dax guffaws. "Have not been to a sex club. Doubt I ever will."

"Will you help me with the other things?"

Dax holds the list in his hand, gaze flitting between me and it. "You know you don't have to do these things to make yourself less boring, right?"

Biting into a piece of bacon, I chew while thinking about what Dax says.

Do I *have* to do these? No, of course not. But it's because of Duncan that I'm going to.

"I know I don't. But this is going to be a new era of

me. A new Chloe. Someone that does what she wants instead of just dreaming about it."

Dax smiles at me. "Are you really going to open your own jewelry store?"

That pulls a huge grin to my face. "Yes. I'm going to make it happen."

It's the one thing I've always loved doing, but never had the courage to make happen. Both Dax and Duncan—even though I hate him now—chased after their dreams of playing hockey.

So why can't I do it?

"Whatever you need, I'll help, Sunshine. We're going to make it happen."

We.

Within a minute, Dax is already plotting how he can help. Duncan? He could never be bothered with it because he was too busy with hockey and trying to get back to the NHL.

Something he still hasn't done.

At least that's gratifying to me.

"Thanks, Dax." I peck his cheek and watch as a blush creeps over his cheeks.

"Don't mention it."

"I'm serious. Your brother never did anything to support me, so it means a lot that I have it from you."

Dax sighs. "I'm sorry my brother wasn't a better guy for you. If I'd have known what he was doing—"

"I know." I pat his arm. "At least I don't have to go through a painful divorce."

"Enough about my brother." Dax gulps down the rest of his coffee. "I was going to suggest a hike after breakfast, but I don't think this weather is going to clear anytime soon."

"I don't think I could take a hike. I'll be lucky to

manage breakfast and going downstairs to the couch. Although…"

Dax groans. "What?"

"If this rain lets up, maybe I could start with skinny-dipping in the lake out back."

"I won't stop you." Dax hops off the bed with all the grace of a professional athlete. "Now, eat up, Sunshine, because I don't want you getting sick on me."

"Yes, Dax."

I watch as he walks out of the room, shaking his head. I stuff another piece of bacon into my mouth and lean back against the headboard. The steady drum of rain against the window could easily pull me back into sleep.

For the first time since I ran out on Duncan, I don't feel the weight of the entire world on my shoulders. And it's all thanks to his brother.

Thank God for Dax, because otherwise, I don't know where I would be right now.

Oh, I do know.

Married to a cheater.

At least that didn't happen. One small win for the day.

Chapter Four

DAX

MARCUS

You've had twelve hours

MARCUS

What the hell is going on?

BODE

Technically, more than twelve hours, Cap

MARCUS

Doesn't matter

MARCUS

My point still stands

JASPER

We want to know what the hell is going on

NOAH

I mean, I did enjoy seeing Duncan's rage face yesterday

NOAH

Fucker deserved it

GRAHAM

But what happened?

BODE

Are you still there, Dax?

BODE

Did you leave the group chat and we missed it?

JASPER

That would require pulling you away from Stevie long enough to notice

BODE

Sorry, I can't help that I'm in love

NOAH

Who would have ever thought you'd say those words?

GRAHAM

Not me

MARCUS

Or me

JASPER

Agreed

BODE

You fuckers suck

BODE

Let me be happy

MARCUS

We are happy for you

GRAHAM

But also, where is Dax?

GRAHAM

He hasn't left the group chat

NOAH

Thankfully it tells you when people do

I laugh, scrolling through the messages from the guys as I plop down onto the couch. It's about the only thing distracting me from Chloe's list.

The list where she apparently wants to go skinny-dipping and have sex with a mustached man at a sex club.

I'm no prude by any means, but I'm not the most… experienced of men, shall we say.

Not when compared to the likes of Bode when he was in his bachelor days.

DAX

I'm fine

MARCUS

Where have you been?

BODE

What happened yesterday?

JASPER

Where'd you run off to?

GRAHAM

And why didn't the wedding happen?

NOAH

You should have seen your brother's face!

OF COURSE NOAH of all people would take the most

delight in seeing Duncan get left at the altar since he cheated on Noah's sister.

> Chloe overhead a conversation that Duncan was having with his girlfriend

NOAH

I'm not surprised

NOAH

But what a fucking asshole

NOAH

I hate him

GRAHAM

To put it mildly

MARCUS

Is she okay?

BODE

That has to hurt

JASPER

Can we find Duncan and punch him?

> Take a number

I CAN'T BELIEVE my brother. Just thinking about what he did to Chloe has my fist tightening. I wish I could have seen his face. He deserves every ounce of pain he got for hurting my best friend like he did.

Not the brotherly thing to be thinking, but when has Duncan ever put anyone besides himself first?

MARCUS

If you two need anything, let us know

MARCUS

We're here for you

BODE

Yeah, whatever we can do

JASPER

Cats are so cool they have their own musical?

NOAH

What the fuck?

NOAH

Why are you talking about cats?

GRAHAM

Did you mean to message us?

MARCUS

Oh God, no one tell the girls about singing cats or I'll have to get them a cat

BODE

Okay, but why is Jasper of all people talking about cats

GRAHAM

He hates everything

NOAH

Well, not hockey

And now Jasper is ghosting us

BODE

Want to bet he thinks if he ignores us long enough, we'll forget about this?

NOAH

Probably

At least until Bode does something stupid

BODE

Hey, nothing stupid from me

BODE

Unless you want to see how cute my kid is, then I can send you all the pictures

BODE

<<picture of Caleb sitting in living room>>

NOAH

He's literally just sitting there, Bode

GRAHAM

What's so special about that?

MARCUS

He is in a Knights onesie looking cute

NOAH

There's that

GRAHAM

Are we going to become these people if we have kids?

GRAHAM

Thinking our kid is cute all the time?

MARCUS

Yes

BODE

You two will be even worse

Every moment of your kid's life will be documented because you two will love it

NOAH

Yeah, we will be annoyingly awesome about having kids

MARCUS

And once again, we've all forgotten that
Jasper is nowhere to be seen now

On that note, I'm going to ghost all of you

BODE

You know you don't actually tell people
you're ghosting them, right?

MARCUS

Clearly Dax has never ghosted anyone in
his life

NOAH

Good man

Just leaving to go hang with Chloe

GRAHAM

How long will you be ghosting us?

GRAHAM

Just so we know?

A week maybe?

BODE

A week? Jesus…what are we going to do
without you, man?

MARCUS

I don't know, maybe hang out with Stevie
and your kid?

BODE

I mean more like him checking in with us to
make sure he's okay

NOAH
Aww

NOAH

What a good dad you are

BODE

NOAH

Love you too

Now I'm really ghosting all of you

GRAHAM

See you soon, Dax

I SHAKE my head as I toss my phone onto the couch cushion next to me. I love these guys. They've become a family to me ever since I was drafted by the Knights. We've been through a lot together, and I know I can depend on them for anything.

The sound of soft footsteps patter overhead followed by the sound of the shower.

What a weird twenty-four hours it's been.

I planned on staying here to while away the time before having to head back to the city for offseason training.

Now, Chloe and I are going to pass the time here together.

Which brings me back to her list.

Have sex at a sex club with a mustached stranger

OUT OF EVERYTHING ON IT, that's the one thing that is sticking in my brain. More like a neon flashing light that

Chloe wants to get out there and have sex with some random stranger.

It's not something I would ever do. Sex means something to me. It always has. I like to give off the whole vibe that I like having sex with people I meet at clubs, but it never actually goes that way.

Before Bode met Stevie, I was his wingman. We'd always chat up the women in bars when traveling. But when it came time to seal the deal? I'd bow out.

Meaningless sex isn't for me. Especially after seeing how my older brother treated women.

I need it to mean more. It's not like I *haven't* had it, but it was fine.

Was it because I was holding out for Chloe? No.

Absolutely not.

But I felt like I was faking it because the feelings weren't there.

"You okay?"

Chloe's standing at the bottom of the stairs in an oversized sweatshirt that hangs off one shoulder and a pair of bike shorts. The cotton material catches the water dripping from her hair.

I shake myself out of my stupor. "Sorry. Just messaging with the guys."

She walks around the couch and takes a seat next to me. "Everything okay with them?"

"They were checking in and seeing how everything is going here."

Chloe winces. "I didn't mean to make people worry about you too."

"They're fine. No one is going to worry because I told them we'll be hanging out here for a week or two."

I hope it's two. I know Chloe isn't in a good headspace

right now, and I'd like to be able to help her get back on her feet.

"You really are a lifesaver, Dax."

"Do I need to buy one if you go skinny-dipping out back?" I laugh.

"Stop." She swats at my chest. "I'm a good swimmer."

"You know how cold that water is? It's not like jumping into a swimming pool."

She straightens her back. "Okay, then. You're going to do it with me."

"Wait, how did this get flipped back on me? I don't have anything to prove."

"You said you wanted to help me with my list, so this will be you helping."

I can feel my dick shrinking into my body at the thought of the freezing-cold water. Even in the summer, it never gets warm. I'm hoping that's one thing she won't want to do.

"Ugh. Why can't I ever say no to you?"

A triumphant grin slides into place. "That's what I was hoping for."

Helping Chloe with her list might be more than I bargained for. How am I going to be able to hide my feelings from her when I'm around her all the time while she's having these new experiences? Aren't these types of things supposed to bring people closer together?

Years of practice and being around Chloe helped put the mask in place, but now that there's no boyfriend to speak of?

I don't know how I'll keep my emotions in check around her.

Chapter Five

CHLOE

I can't sit still. Pacing around the bedroom of the cabin, it's hard to keep the antsy thoughts at bay. It's only been a few days, but being out in the middle of the woods is making me stir-crazy.

I've never been one to sit around. I thought spending time with Dax at his home away from home would be just what I needed to clear my head and get past my fiasco of a wedding.

Turns out, I might need to get a move on with my list. Give me something to focus on instead of the repetitive cycle of thoughts.

Wedding. Duncan. Cheating. Running away. Wedding. Duncan. Cheating. Running away.

Rinse and repeat.

Is hiding out really going to solve any of my problems? Will my list help?

No. But it will help me feel better.

The high-pitched trill of my phone echoes through the tiny cabin. Glancing at the screen where it sits on the bed, I see it's my mom calling.

Again.

Sighing, I know I can't ignore her much longer.

It's been three days since I ran out, and the only person I've seen or talked to is Dax. Which is how I like it.

Sliding my thumb across the bottom of the screen, I answer. "Hi, Mom."

"That's all you have to say to me? 'Hi, Mom' after you ran away from your fiancé?"

I swallow down the annoyance that threatens to spill over. It's not like she knows the reason why. The only person who does is Dax. Well, Duncan should be able to figure it out, but I doubt he has.

"I could have sent you to voicemail."

"Chloe Ann Davis. Is that any way to treat your mother? I've been worried sick about you."

"Look, Mom, I'm sorry, okay? I overheard a conversation Duncan was having and I couldn't marry him."

"What could you have possibly heard to make you run out on your wedding? You were so happy."

"He was cheating on me!" I hiss. "How could I marry someone that can't be faithful to me?"

"Cheating? I'm sure he wasn't cheating. Duncan loves you."

"Does he?" I spit out. "Because it sure sounded like he loves this other person more."

"Nonsense, Chloe." I can picture my mom—blonde hair fixed back in a neat bun, lips pursed together. "You must have misunderstood him."

"Hard to misunderstand someone when they say 'I love you' to someone else."

"And what if it was his mother?"

Now I can picture her quirking her brow at me. The same way she did when I was a kid and she was trying to figure out if I was lying or not.

"Why would he be on the phone with his mom before the wedding? I wouldn't be calling you."

"That would require you to answer your phone if I called."

"Mom." I give her an aggrieved sigh.

"There's still time to make this right. Duncan has oh so generously said he would still marry you if you come back."

"Oh he will, will he?"

"You don't have to be so childish," Mom snaps. "You need to be an adult about this situation. Who cares if he's cheating? Duncan can provide you with the kind of life you've always dreamed of."

"A cheating husband is the kind of life I've always dreamed about?"

"Chloe, I expect you back here at the house by Saturday at noon so the wedding-"

"Well, I'm sorry to tell you, *Mom*, that that will absolutely not be happening. I have no intentions of marrying Duncan. And since you seem to be in contact with him, you can tell him to fuck off!"

I hang up, feeling more frustrated than before. Should I have spoken to my mother like that? Probably not.

But when she puts Duncan's well-being before mine and thinks she knows what's best for me? I really don't care.

I toss the phone onto the bed and storm downstairs. Dax is working out in front of the TV. Dax has been in my life longer than he hasn't been in it. No matter what is going on in my life, Dax is always there for me.

So seeing him like this? Working out in his living room in only a pair of shorts and tennis shoes?

It's something I've seen before. But the butterflies in my stomach that it's conjuring up? That's a new feeling.

Sweat clings to his bare chest. His abs and biceps flex as he squats and thrusts his arms over his head. The hockey charm necklace I made him when he first got drafted—a set of crossed hockey sticks with number fourteen on it—hangs around his neck.

I shouldn't like looking at him like this. Ogling him, more like it.

It's only because I'm in such an emotional state that this is happening. That has to be it.

This is Dax. My best friend. My ex-fiancé's brother. I cannot be having *feelings* for him.

"You okay?"

Dax's voice breaks me out of my thoughts.

"What? Umm, yeah."

I shake myself out of my stupor.

"You don't seem it."

He grabs the towel from the mantel and drags it over his face and down his chest. I shouldn't be watching the movement, but I am.

A single bead of sweat trails down the path between his pecs. Really nice pecs, I'm now discovering.

"Chloe?" Dax says again. "You sure you're okay?"

"I'm fine." This time, I swing my gaze to meet his and don't let my eyes betray me. "Just had a conversation with my mom."

"Ahh." He tosses the towel down and walks around to me. "Tells me all I need to know."

I nod. "Apparently if I show up to her place by Saturday at noon, Duncan will still be willing to marry me."

"What? Are you going to do it?" he asks, shock lacing his voice.

Shaking my head, I make up my mind on the only thing I want to do. "I'm going skinny-dipping."

"What?" Dax looks confused now at my one-eighty.

"The only thing I want to do right now is start on my list. And that means I'm going skinny-dipping."

Throwing open the French doors, I jog down the steps that lead to the dock. Sunlight sneaks through the high treetops as leaves and sticks crunch under my feet. Steam rises from the rain that's finally stopped after the last few days.

"Wait," Dax calls out after me.

"No. I'm tired of everyone thinking they know what's best for me. I'm starting this with or without your help."

When the trees break, a small lake appears with a tiny dock that extends from the edge of the water.

I breathe in the clean air, letting it fill my lungs as I tug my T-shirt over my head.

"Jesus, Chloe. Warn a man."

Dax draws up short behind me. When I turn around, his hand is covering his eyes.

"I told you I was doing this. Not sure how else I should warn you. Are you going to do this with me or not?"

"I...I guess I'm going to do it with you."

"You could sound more excited."

I shimmy out of my shorts and chuck them his way. They fall in a heap at his feet as he peeks at them.

"Is it weird we're going to see each other naked?" he asks, voice quieter than I've ever heard it before.

I give it a thought as I unhook my bra and slide it from my arms. "How about I jump in first and then close my eyes and then you jump in?"

"Fine."

Taking off my underwear, I don't think twice before I jump into the lake. I try not to suck in water as the cold feels like thousands of tiny needles pricking my skin.

Erupting out of the water, I get a flash of Dax jumping in on the other side.

He shoots up out of the water, teeth already chattering.

"Holy shit! Why did you let me do this?"

"You could have said no." I splash water his way. "Besides, you're all sweaty after your workout. It should feel nice."

"There's refreshing, Sunshine, then there's jumping into sub-Arctic water."

"It's not that cold."

Dax swims closer, water clinging to his hair. "Your lips turning blue say otherwise."

"They are not."

As I tread water, the sun beats down overhead, warming my face. The trees rustle in the wind. Pushing onto my back, I swim farther into the lake.

There is something entirely freeing about being stark naked in the middle of a lake. Having been to Dax's cabin before, I know others live around here. It's not just *his* lake. Any one of them could happen upon us out here.

But I don't care.

That's half the excitement of it.

"Okay, I want to move out here so I can do this all the time. I don't know why you've never done it."

"Who says I haven't?"

I peek one eye at Dax, swimming closer to me. The water is murky at best, but it doesn't do much to hide our bodies. Flipping onto my stomach, I aim for some modesty. I don't need Dax seeing everything.

"I feel like you would have told me already when I made the list."

Dax laughs. "I was too distracted by the fact you want to go to a sex club."

"Have you done this?" I ask, ignoring his comment.

"No. I guess I'm boring like you."

"Should we make a 'Dax needs to not be boring' list too?"

This time, it's Dax splashing me. "I don't need a list to know I'm boring. I'm happy with my life as it is."

"You play for the Knights. That's about as un-boring as it gets."

"Which is why I like my life as it is," he says. "No more excitement is needed."

I point a finger his way, swimming closer. "Except for the excitement you're going to help me with, right?"

"Do you remember when you came to look at that one school with me?" Dax asks. "The one I didn't go to, but my parents couldn't come with me because Duncan had something more important?"

The memory of that day is so vivid. Duncan has always come first with their parents, and I hate it. Dax has always been living in his older brother's shadow—whether with his family or the NHL. It's like he's never been good enough.

"How could I forget?"

"You made us a road-trip playlist, bought us the worst kinds of snacks, and made it the best day. I still love peach rings because of that trip."

"And we took the most ridiculous pictures around campus. I think they would have barred you from the school on that alone."

Dax smiles at me. "That's why I want to do this with you."

This is why Dax has always been my best friend. With Duncan, I felt like I had to act a certain way. Tone my real self down for him. It's not until I left him that I realized just how much I was doing to make him love me.

Dax? Dax loves me without question. In the best friend

kind of way. We've always been our real selves with each other.

Singing bad songs at the top of our lungs. Rescuing each other when we need it. Helping with lists.

Dax might think I'm crazy for doing this, but he will be there right alongside me every step of the way.

That's what I need in a partner—if I ever decide to leave the single life behind. Duncan has scarred me for life. How the hell am I ever going to trust another man, other than Dax?

"Okay, I need to get out before everything on me freezes off."

"You're such a baby." I laugh.

"Well, I want to protect the important parts. Close your eyes while I get out."

"Okay."

I make a show of covering my eyes with my hand so I can't see him. When the sloshing of water hits my ears followed by Dax cursing, I can't help but peek between my fingers.

"Are you okay?" I ask.

Dax has one leg on the metal ladder, trying to climb it. With his bare ass on full display.

"Shit. I'm fine. Just slipped."

"Do you need help?"

"No!" he shouts. "I mean, I'm good. Totally fine."

"You sure?"

"Are you looking?" he fires back.

"No." I smack my hand back over my eyes. Holy shit. How come I have never noticed how nice of an ass my best friend has?

There were times Duncan and I were broken up over some stupid fight. Dax was always there for me, but always only as my friend. I guess I never let myself notice him. Because wow.

You could bounce quarters off that ass.

"You better not be," Dax calls out.

There's no point in letting him know I'm looking. I'm his best friend. He doesn't see me as anything other than that.

"No. I promise."

"Good."

Taking a deep breath, I sink under the surface of the lake. I let the cold water flow around me. I need it to quell the thoughts about Dax's ass.

Not something I need to be thinking about. It's only because I'm in such a bad headspace right now.

That's it. Nothing else.

I'll let myself have that peek and move on.

It won't be hard, right?

Chapter Six

DAX

That was a really bad idea. A very bad idea. In the whole universe of bad ideas, skinny-dipping with my best friend that I'm secretly in love with? That's at the top of the list.

Fuck. I really shouldn't have done that.

Picking up my bag, I toss it over my shoulder and head toward my truck.

After our dip in the lake, we had a quiet few days.

Playing games. Watching movies. Cooking dinner together.

The weather turned to rain again, so there wasn't much we could do besides stay inside. It's one of the things I love most about being around Chloe. The easy silences.

We're never straining to fill them.

Throwing my duffel into the car and standing next to the driver's door, I remind myself to switch my focus to the team's upcoming training and offseason practices.

It'll be the distraction I need to keep from thinking about Chloe.

But it's hard not to think about that little sliver of skin I saw on the side of her chest as I went into the water. Because even that tiny inch of skin has me thinking of everything I want to do to her. Things that I *can't* do to her.

Even though she's officially done with my brother—and sworn off all men—she'll always be Duncan's ex.

Which makes me hate my brother even more because I'll never get Chloe that way.

"You ready?"

Chloe's jogging down the front steps of my cabin, bag in hand. In a pair of overalls, with her hair swept into a messy contraption on top of her head, she looks better than I've seen her in days.

"Waiting on you, Sunshine."

Chloe smiles at me, dark sunglasses hiding her eyes.

"I'm not ready to go back to the real world." She sighs, shaking her head. "I wish we could stay here forever."

"If only I didn't have to go back for hockey."

"Hey." Chloe nudges me and throws her bag into the back of the SUV. "You have to win the cup. I've been waiting too long to see you lift it."

I beam back at her. "I'm planning on it."

"Good. You can focus on that. I'll have to find an apartment."

Firing the truck up, I point it in the direction of the main road. "You know, you can stay with me as long as you need."

"I can't. You know I can't."

I peek one eye over at her, and she's picking at her nail. "Says who?"

She drops her hands into her lap. "I have to move on, Dax."

"Move on from me?" There's a panic in my voice as the car swerves a little too hard around the corner.

"No. God, no." She reaches over and squeezes my arm

resting on the center console. "But if I keep mooching off you, it's just going to delay me moving on from your brother."

I blow out a breath as the sunlight peeks into the cab from the passing trees. "Good. But you know the offer is always there."

"You're the best, Dax. Truly. I don't know if I would have survived these last few days without you."

"You would have. You're stronger than you think."

"I probably would have gone back and married him." She shudders.

"Well, now you get to find a new place to live and start over."

"Care to help me look?" Chloe asks.

"Of course."

That earns me a genuine smile from her. It's one of the smiles she saves just for me. It has my heart flailing around in my chest. God, why couldn't I feel this way about someone else? But no matter how hard I tried to move on from Chloe, it was always her. All the way back to high school.

Until I asked my dick of a brother for advice on how to ask her out and he did it instead. It's around that time I started hating my brother for getting what I wanted. He didn't deserve her then and he still doesn't deserve her now.

"Whatever I find won't be anything fancy. I don't have much of a budget."

"And what is your budget?"

"Cheap."

Chloe plugs in her phone, tapping a few things before the first few notes of an old pop song come on.

"Our playlist?"

She nods, starting to sing along. "I had to recreate it."

Chloe cranks the volume, bopping along to the song and singing—terribly, I might add.

"I forgot how bad you are." I laugh.

That only makes her sing louder, dancing in the seat.

"C'mon, Dax." She pokes me in the side. "You know you want to sing along."

"I'm the worst singer in the world."

"I don't care." She pokes me again. "C'mon."

I wait a beat before busting out with the chorus. It has Chloe holding out a pretend microphone to me as I focus on the road and the song.

God, this is what I love about being with her. How it's always been. Things are light and fun. Right now, it's just the two of us. There's no worrying about what's to come. And I know Chloe has a lot of those concerns right now.

"I forgot how bad we sound together." Chloe reaches over and turns the volume down. "Remind me that we should never go on tour."

"Done." I laugh. "I'm not giving up my day job anytime soon."

"Meanwhile, I'm trying to find one."

"No luck with that boutique you tried calling?"

She shakes her head. "She already filled the position. I called a few other places, but if nothing pans out, I might be going all in on Charms by Chloe."

"Is that what you're calling it?" I sneak a quick peek at her, grinning.

"Is it too kitschy? I mean, I've been toying around with some ideas."

Pulling out her notebook, she flips a few pages. Idea after idea is scrawled on the page. Some circled, others crossed out.

"I like Chloe's Creations, but I don't know. Charms by Chloe sounds better to me."

"A certain charm if you will." I wink at her.

"Well, I might already have a logo in mind too. I just need to find someone to help me design it."

I wince, thinking about how much that is going to cost. "Can I ask you the question you might not want to hear?"

"How am I going to pay for it?"

I nod. "Sorry. I know it's expensive to start your own business."

She picks at a loose thread in a rip in her overalls. "I figure if I sell my engagement ring, that'll help cover my costs for a few months. Maybe start designing and creating and selling everything online."

"I think that's a great idea. And you know…"

Chloe swats me on the arm. "I am not living with you to save money. If I get desperate, maybe."

"I'll see if Marcus's wife or Bode's girlfriend might have any contacts you could start selling with."

"Doesn't Marcus's wife work at a school?"

"Yeah, but don't moms love stuff like that? Charms for their kids' birthdays? I know my mom always had one."

"Not a bad idea." The sound of her pen against the paper fills the cab of the truck. "You'll have to send me their numbers. If they wouldn't mind."

"I don't think they would," I say.

"You sure? I know I'm not officially a part of the WAGS crew."

"Maybe you can start a BFs crew."

"Really?" She laughs. "Best friends crew?"

"What? It can be a thing."

"Considering I'll never be a WAG, that's for sure."

I keep my reaction to myself. "No WAG. Got it."

"All men, for that matter right now. Never a hockey player again. After Duncan, I don't want to take that chance."

"Hey, we're not all bad."

"You're different, Dax. You're one of the kindest people on the planet. Your brother? Not so much. He always had excuses as to why we were partly exclusive."

"Partly exclusive?" I question. That's the first I'm hearing of this.

"Yeah. Always exclusive when he was in town. But if he was gone training with other teams or when he was in Europe that one summer before he joined Colorado, we weren't exclusive."

"I could murder him," I grumble.

"I guess it was his excuse to sleep with whoever he wanted." She smacks herself on the head. "I seriously can't believe how naïve I was."

"He knows just what to say to keep you on the hook. Trust me, I always thought he was going to help me become a better skater and he never did."

She scoffs. "That's because you're already a better player."

"Nice try."

The truck grows silent as the farmlands around the city pass us by. I wish I was the better player, but I've always been in my big brother's shadow.

Since I started playing in the NHL, I've always been compared to him. He had a natural talent that he never had to work at. Me? It was a grind every day to get where I am now. I wish I had that same skill, but I don't. In high school, I wanted to be just like my big brother. The way he carried himself on the ice and how easily it came to him.

Now? All I want is to stop being compared to him.

"Does it help that you're a better person?" Chloe pulls me from my thoughts.

"A little." I hold up my thumb and forefinger a few

centimeters apart. "Wouldn't hurt if I could have a cup to show for it."

"You'll get one. I know."

Chloe squeezes my forearm before going back to her notebook. The same notebook that her damn list is in.

My focus this season needs to be on the team and improving where I am to help us actually finish in the play-offs. I don't need to be worrying about her swearing off all men.

I'll never have Chloe. I need to accept that. Having her as my best friend is all I'll ever get.

And that needs to be good enough for me.

Chapter Seven

"**A**re you sure he's not here?" I ask again.

"Yes."

"Positive?"

Pulling up to the security gate, we get buzzed in without question.

"At least the security guards still like you." Dax laughs.

"Probably more than Duncan."

Each house is bigger than the last as we drive to the back of the neighborhood. I don't know why I ever thought I would be happy in a place like this. It's about as opposite me as the sun and the moon.

All I want is a house with enough rooms for a family—*one day*—and a space to create.

Dax laughs as the ostentatious house that was once mine comes into view. Well, partially mine. It's not like there's much in the way of my things here. When Duncan asked me to move in, I put most of my belongings in storage. Sold off the furniture I had, because why would I need it? My primary focus then became planning our wedding, which didn't leave time for much else.

"You're growling," Dax tells me.

"Ugh. Sorry. Just frustrated that I'm moving into a new apartment and have nothing."

"Sorry." Dax pats my knee. I ignore the warmth that spreads through my body at the slight touch. Ever since I got the tiniest peek of his ass at the lake, it's all I've been thinking about.

Who knew your best friend's ass could be a great distraction from your fiancé cheating on you?

"Besides," Dax continues, "my mom said he used the honeymoon tickets since you, in her words, refused to marry him."

"Refused?" My voice gets abnormally high and shrieky. Something I'm finding happening more and more often. "I can't believe her. Refused!"

"Just be thankful we can be in and out today without having to see him."

"There's that," I grumble.

My nerves ratchet up as Dax parks in the circular drive. The all-black façade shines in the sunlight. A fountain burbles in front of the gray front door. All the curtains are drawn as I fish my key out of my purse.

"You sure you don't want to stay here?" Dax jogs past me, grabbing the key from my hand and opening the front door. "Who wouldn't love all of this?"

The entryway might be the most unwelcoming space I've ever been in. Solid black marble with a stone statue in the center greets us.

"Who looks at this and says they want it?" I curl my lip up in disgust at the horrible sculpture. "And he said I had no taste."

"C'mon." Dax grabs my elbow and steers me upstairs. "Let's get your stuff and get out of here. It wouldn't surprise me if a ghost lived here."

I snicker as he walks up the equally garish stairs. "His name is Ralph."

"Oh, you have a ghost then?" Dax smiles at me as I lead us toward the bedroom.

I nod. "Very friendly. Probably the only thing I'd want to take with me that wasn't mine."

Stepping into the main bedroom, I draw up short. It's a mess. Sheets are in heaps at the foot of the bed. A half-drunk bottle of champagne sits on the nightstand. And lying in the center? A red, lacy thong.

"I cannot believe him!" I storm into the room, heading straight for the closet. All of my clothes are in piles. "He thinks *I* was in the wrong for running out on him? When he clearly has already moved on?"

Grabbing my clothes, I chuck them behind me and start ripping things off the hangers. I can't help it.

The man cheats on me and has the nerve to say if I come back, he'll still marry me? Then moves someone else in here when I don't come back?

"What. An. Asshole."

I pull all of his clothes out of drawers. Pull every last one of Duncan's precious sneakers from their place of honor on the shelves.

He probably loved them more than he loved me.

"Hey." Dax grabs my hand before I can start in on whoever's clothes now take up the small space where mine were. "Is this helpful?"

I glare up at him, letting out a deep breath. "Yes. How are you related to someone so terrible?"

"I don't claim him." Dax smiles at me, before pulling me in for a comforting hug.

"I wouldn't either."

I wrap my arms around Dax and let his strength keep me standing. How did I let myself get so taken by someone like Duncan? Did I really think I couldn't find someone better? Someone who treated me right?

When we got back together before getting engaged, my mom pushed me to lock him down. I guess she got into my head more than I thought. Telling me I wouldn't find anyone as good as Duncan.

More like she wanted me to be financially secure. But when I was with Duncan, he was always so sincere in what he said and did that it was hard *not* to believe him that he loved me.

Joke's on me, I guess.

"Okay." I push out of Dax's arms, his cologne washing over me. The same cologne that he's used for years. The clean, manly scent I always teased him about using too much of in high school. "Okay, no more thinking about Duncan. Let's get my stuff and get out of here."

"Without destroying the place, Sunshine." Dax taps my nose. "I don't want to have to bail you out of jail."

"Would be something good for my list." I laugh.

"No," Dax deadpans. "I want you to stay boring if it means you don't get arrested."

Grabbing one of the boxes we brought in, I start piling clothes in it. I don't care that they're a mess. I just want to get out of here.

"Fine. No jail time. But I'm selling the jewelry he gave me. Is that fair?"

He nods. "More than fair."

Dax and I sort through the mess I made—something that made it harder in hindsight to go through everything —and get all of my clothes into three of the boxes. A few pairs of shoes take up box number four, with a few knickknacks, jewelry, and picture frames filling the last box. They're all piled onto my purple chair that now sits in the middle of the messy room.

"Is it pathetic that all of my worldly possession can fit into five boxes?"

Dax smiles. "Technically your chair doesn't fit in a box."

"Stop it." I swat at his chest.

"Hey. You'll get all of your furniture when you move into your new place and can decorate however you want."

"Think I should take the stone statue?" I laugh.

"Only if you plan on destroying it to use in your jewelry."

That pulls more laughter out of me. "I don't think I could pay people to buy stuff with that god-awful stone in it."

Dax looks around as we carry the boxes downstairs. "He really is full of himself."

Photos of Duncan line the walls. Photos of him playing hockey. Various sponsor photoshoots. Ones from before he was dropped after it came out he was sleeping with the coach's wife.

We weren't together at that point. One of the longer stretches we were broken up. But he said he didn't know the woman he was sleeping with was married.

God. I feel like such an idiot for having taken him back.

It takes us two trips to get everything in the back of the truck before we head back to Dax's house.

A house that I love. With a wooden exterior painted blue and white, the front porch and overhead balcony are decorated with various flowerpots. My doing, to make it more welcoming.

All the walls are painted a light gray with soft rugs on top of the refinished hardwood floors. Every bit of Dax's house is what it should be.

Soft.

Warm.

Open.

It's perfect, I think as we're pulling into the three-car garage.

"Want to leave everything in here?" Dax asks, turning the truck off.

"Sounds good to me." I unbuckle my seatbelt and hop out. "Want me to order pizza?"

"I can get it," Dax says.

I shake my head. "Absolutely not. You're helping me move. It's the least I can do."

"As long as you get—"

"Thai chicken," I finish. "I know. With breadsticks and cheese sauce."

He beams back at me. "It's like you know me or something."

"Only for a year or two," I joke. "I'm going to go get cleaned up before it gets here."

"Sounds good. I'm going to get a quick workout in."

"Sorry moving my boxes didn't help."

"If you need help moving your furniture around, that might count as a workout." Dax winks, turning to head toward his weight room in the back of the house.

"Hey, Dax?"

"Yeah?" He stops, leaning against the wall.

Bounding over, I rest a hand on his forearm to press onto my toes and peck his cheek. "Thank you. I wouldn't have made it through any of this without you."

The tender look Dax aims my way sends my thoughts spiraling. Nothing but care and kindness. "You know I'm always here for you, Sunshine. Whatever you need."

"You're the best friend anyone could ever have. If they gave out trophies, you'd get number one every time."

This time, Dax returns the kiss on my cheek before

leaving and pulling the door closed behind him. I'm standing in the middle of the hall, glued to the floor.

I can feel the imprint of his lips on my cheek. The soft skin of his jaw as it brushed against mine. My skin tingles with awareness from the brief touch.

What in the world is going on?

Dax and I have always been affectionate with one another. It's never affected me in the past, so why is this time different?

It must be all the emotions still bubbling over inside of me. That *has* to be it. There's no other explanation.

Because this is Dax we're talking about. I absolutely cannot be having feelings for him. Feelings for Dax would make everything messy and complicated. After running out on his brother, the last thing I want is complicated.

Hell, at this point, I don't even know if I want anything new, let alone complicated. If I do, it needs to be easy. A nice guy who treats me better than Duncan.

Doesn't Dax treat you better than Duncan ever has?

I ignore the voice in my head and phone in the pizza order.

I don't need to be thinking about how well Dax treats me. It's a moot point because I've sworn off all men for good.

Including Dax.

Chapter Eight

DAX

Fuck. That feels good. Really damn good. It's not like I ignore my workouts during offseason, but I've spent more time than usual outside of the gym.

With Chloe.

Once she started planning her wedding, I happily spent every spare second in the gym training when I wasn't helping her. It helped get my mind off her nuptials.

This summer? I've wanted to spend my time with her.

Not that anything is going to happen with her. But a guy can want to hang out with his best friend, right?

I would run, she would work on her jewelry, and we'd hang out at night together. Have dinner. Low-key things that *friends* do together.

With offseason activities officially starting, it marks the end of summer.

The plates clank together as I finish my set, dropping my elbows onto my knees. My sweaty T-shirt clings to my chest. A few of the guys are on the treadmills, but since it's not an official practice, not too many people are here.

"You ready for the season?" Jasper asks as he strolls in, hitting me with a towel.

Glancing down at my watch, I see that he's on time. For him, that's late. On our first day of offseason training, Jasper is usually the first person in the locker room.

"Are you?"

"Why wouldn't I be?"

"You're late."

He rolls his eyes at me. "I'm on time."

"Which is late for you," I clarify.

Jasper flips me off as Bode walks in.

"Why are you pissing off the old man already?" Bode laughs.

"He's on time."

Bode eyes me before swinging his gaze back to Jasper.

"Are you feeling okay? You're never late."

"I'm on time." He pushes a frustrated hand through his hair. "Sue me. I slept in a little longer today."

"But you never do," Bode says. "Are you sick? Do we need to be worried?"

"Seriously, fuck off." Jasper flips off Bode this time.

"Someone's getting cranky in their old age," Noah jokes as he joins us from the treadmill.

"I'm the same age as you."

Noah waggles his eyebrows at him. "Yeah, but I have a boyfriend. He keeps me young."

"That's your secret?" Jasper crosses his arms over his chest. "Dating someone younger than you to keep you from feeling old?"

"Doesn't hurt."

"Weren't you just in the ice bath?" Bode throws back at him.

"Just because I feel young, doesn't mean my body can't

do with some good old-fashioned therapy before we start the season," Noah says.

I move to the free weights, starting bicep curls as Noah and Bode argue about getting old. Looking in the mirror, I notice Jasper smiling down at his phone. Something that he would have yelled at us about having in the training room, but he doesn't seem to mind.

Something is definitely going on with him.

It's then that Noah notices. "Hey! You can't have your phone in here."

"What?" Jasper looks like he got caught with his hand in the cookie jar. "I was texting my massage therapist."

"No one looks that happy texting their 'massage therapist,'" Noah says, adding air quotes around the words.

"Unless you're Bode," Jasper deflects.

He shakes his head, starting his own set of reps. "Nope. Stevie is an aesthetician. Big difference."

"You couldn't have thrown me a bone?" Jasper whines.

"You needs a bone?" Marcus asks, coming into the locker room with Graham.

"Maybe if Jasper got a different kind of bone, he wouldn't be so grumpy," Noah whispers.

Not all that quietly because we all hear him.

"I'm going to kick your ass." Jasper punches him in the shoulder.

"That's not my ass." Noah grins back at him.

"Just you wait. When we're done in here, it's going to happen."

"If you can catch me." He winks at him before dodging out of Jasper's reach.

"Can you two behave? I'm not at home. I don't want to have to discipline you for behaving like children," Marcus tells them. "Why can't you be mature like Bode? Or Dax?"

I burst out laughing. "Who knew Bode and I would be the mature ones around here?"

Marcus takes one of the empty treadmills and starts his workout. "You've always been mature. Bode is a new development."

"What can I say? Being a father does that to you."

The dopey grin on his face tells us all he loves it. After discovering he had an eight-month-old son last year, he quit the playboy lifestyle and gave everything up for him. Even falling in love in the process.

That thought stings. All of the guys are starting to fall in love and find partners that are perfect for them.

Noah and Graham.

Marcus and Harper.

Bode and Stevie.

Hell, even Jasper is suspiciously happy.

When will it be my turn? At some point, I'm going to have to move on from Chloe and find someone to love. I don't know if it will ever be the same, but I have to at least try.

Because she is adamant that she never wants to date another player. I could retire, but I don't think that's the point.

"You good?"

Bode elbows me in the side.

"What?" I look at him in the mirrored wall of the weight room. "Yeah, I'm good."

"You were spacing out there for a minute."

I smile at him. "What did I miss? Noah giving Jasper shit?"

"You've been relatively quiet this summer. What have you been up to?" Bode asks.

"Yeah. You hightail it out of your brother's wedding and it's like you're ghosting us."

Jasper snickers behind me.

"I didn't ghost you guys. I texted you the next day," I remind them.

"Only because we were bugging you," Bode says.

"And I responded."

"Have you been spending all this time with Chloe?" Marcus gives me a cautious eye.

"Not all of it."

They don't need to know that it's an outright lie. But they know my feelings, so I know one of them will call my bluff.

"Is she doing better after everything went down?" Bode asks instead.

Huh. They never drop anything, so it surprises me Bode sidestepped my answer.

"Yeah. She got her own place and is working on starting her own jewelry business," I say.

"Wow. Good for her," Noah says. "Good thing to distract yourself with after being dumped."

I point a finger at him as I move to another weight machine to start leg exercises. "Technically, she dumped him."

"Because he was cheating." Noah rolls his eyes at me. "The same old Duncan. Only caring about himself and getting his dick wet."

"Are we allowed to say that around Dax?" Graham whispers to Noah.

Noah pats him on the cheek. "You don't know how to whisper. And Dax knows it."

"Do I ever."

On the one hand, if it hadn't happened, Duncan and Chloe would be married right now. On the other, at least Chloe is single. Not that she ever wants to date a player again, but there might be a one percent chance in the next five-to-ten years she changes her mind.

Slim, but there's a chance.

Again, another reason I need to move on.

"What are you going to do about it?" Jasper asks.

"What do you mean?" My brows furrow as I look at him, pushing the plate on the leg bar to work my hammies.

"You have feelings for her, right?" Jasper looks at me like I'm the idiot for not knowing this. "Are you just going to let her get away?"

"Right now? Yes."

I start counting my reps to myself to not have to look at any of the guys. This is so not the conversation I thought we'd be having right now.

"Really? I would've thought you would have made a move on her by now," Bode says.

"She just got out of a relationship. Give her some time," Marcus says. "I have a feeling she'll come around."

"Really?" That has me stopping and sitting up. "Why would she want to date her ex-fiancé's brother? She's sworn off all men and hockey players."

"Ouch." They all answer at the same time.

"You have an uphill road ahead of you," Jasper says, "but love is worth it."

"Okay, did I miss something?" Bode sets his weights on the floor and rests his hands on his hips. "Why is Jasper all loved up?"

"The list of whose ass I need to kick keeps growing," Jasper fires back. "I can want my teammate to be happy."

"No, I want to know more about this too," I agree. Anything to get the heat off of me and my *very slim chance* with Chloe.

"There's nothing to tell." Jasper finds one of the treadmills, jacking up the speed to ignore all of us.

"There's definitely something to tell," Marcus says.

"Hey, if he doesn't want to talk, we can leave him alone," I say.

"Want to talk about your love life then?" Bode asks.

"Why don't we talk about if Noah and Graham are going to get married?" I deflect.

"Seriously?" Noah whines. "What is with all the love talk today?"

"You started it." Bode gives him a satisfied grin. "Only right you have to deal with it too."

"Noah wants to win a Stanley Cup together before he proposes," Graham answers for him.

"And I didn't want to say it so I don't jinx anything." Noah rolls his eyes, but he has the same look on his face as the rest of the guys.

That same happy, in love with the best person in the world face.

Does my face look like that when I think about Chloe? Staring at myself in the mirror, I answer my own question.

Yeah, it does.

And it fucking sucks when the person you love most in the world has no idea how you feel.

And will never know if she has anything to say about it.

Being in love sucks.

Chapter Nine

CHLOE

"Not bad if I do say so myself," I say out loud to no one.

Inspecting the newly soldered ring, I'm happy with how it turned out. Considering I've messed up the first three, and nearly burned myself again, the fact that it's a ring?

Yeah, I'm pretty proud of it.

When I decided to go all in on this jewelry-making business, I knew it would be hard. I loved getting to create things like this back in high school, but I didn't think about the learning curve.

At least this one resembles a circle. I guess the tenth time is the charm. Now to figure out how to get the gemstone on it.

Having been in my own studio apartment for two months now, I've finally found the best setup for jewelry making. There wasn't enough room for a kitchen table between the half wall that separated my bedroom space and the kitchen. The living room barely fits my small love seat and coffee table.

A pop-up card table isn't ideal for starting my own business, but it's what I'm working with.

Before I can sort everything out for the next part of the tutorial—thank God for others on the Internet that know how to do it—a knock echoes around my small studio.

Swinging open the front door, my friend Erica rushes into my apartment, dropping her bag on the loveseat.

She greets me with a massive hug. "You're alive!"

"Of course I am. Why wouldn't I be?"

"Oh, I don't know. Maybe because all I got from you after the wedding was 'I need to lie low' and that was it?"

Erica swings her gorgeous, long black hair over her shoulder, piercing me with a knowing look.

"Hey." I point a finger at her. "I texted you my new address."

"Only because I bugged you about where you were living."

I close the door behind her as she plops down onto the couch.

"Well, surprise. Here it is."

She looks around the small space. "You know, you could have stayed with me."

I shake my head. "You and Dax keep saying that."

"I have more than enough room."

"I know." I nod. "But I want a fresh start on my own."

Erica is one of my closest girlfriends here in Nashville. Nothing like my relationship with Dax, but I love her. She's a trust-fund baby—her words—and has a townhouse right in the heart of the city. It's something I wish I could have, but I don't.

I get a small studio apartment until I can make something of myself.

"You sure? It's within walking distance to a lot of great places."

Walking into the kitchen, I grab two bottles of water from the fridge, passing one over to her as I take a seat next to her.

"I'm good. Since I'm not working right now, I don't need to be in the city."

"Any luck finding a job?" she asks.

"Not yet."

"Really? I could try at the boutique."

I shake my head. "Already called. Too many employees right now."

"Ugh. I'm sorry, babe."

"Considering I can't get a job at my friend's place of work, I'm not holding out much hope. But I sold the engagement ring from Duncan, and that will help me get by for now."

Erica whistles. "Damn. I didn't realize he shelled out so much for it."

I smile at her before gulping down my water. "Yup. Should've known when it took up half my finger."

"At least you can figure out what you want to do until then."

"I don't need to figure it out. I already have a plan. Want to see?" I leap up, heading toward the small table.

"Of course you have a plan." She smiles at me. "What is it?"

"I'm finally going to start my jewelry-making business."

"You are?"

"It's slow going," I tell her, "but I'll get there."

"Is that why you haven't been texting me then?"

"Hey." I elbow her in the side. "I've been busy trying to get the rest of my life started."

"And you know, running out on your wedding."

"Best decision ever," I say. "That and giving up on men."

"You are?" Erica takes one of the half-finished rings and inspects it. "This is really good."

"I'm getting there," I tell her, picking up one of the trays of silver solder so she can sit down. "But yes, I'm giving up on men. How can I ever trust any of them not to cheat on me?"

"Sweetheart, Duncan isn't all men."

"Might as well be," I huff.

"Not all men," she reiterates. "There's plenty of good options out there for you. Like Dax."

"Dax? He's my best friend."

She scoffs. "I know that. But have you ever, you know, thought about more with him?"

I drop the tray of silver solder and it scatters across the table and floor. "I just got out of a relationship, Erica. Why would I be thinking about another one?"

Dropping to her knees, she helps me pick up the pieces. "Duncan was terrible. We all knew it, but you were so taken with him, it was hard to get through to you. Dax isn't like that."

"I know that."

"Something to consider."

I drop back onto my ass, crossing my legs in front of me. "Why are you even bringing this up?"

"Honey, Duncan is a douchebag. The worst kind of man because he tells you what you want to hear to get his way. You deserve someone so much better. Someone like Dax."

"Someone *like* Dax or *Dax*?"

Erica throws her hands up. "It doesn't have to be Dax, but since you've sworn off all men…"

"I regret telling you where I live."

"No, you don't." She blows a kiss at me. "You have to have someone tell you the hard things."

My phone buzzes in my pocket and I pull it out.

"Speaking of men." I roll my eyes and show her my phone

DUNCAN

Baby, I miss you

This has gone on long enough

Can we talk?

Please?

I love you

"HAVE YOU TALKED TO HIM?" Erica hands me back my phone.

"No. I don't know if I could do it without screaming at him."

"You need to do it, babe. You need closure."

"I hate that you're right."

"I'm always right." She winks at me.

"But what if he pulls me back in? Says just the right things to convince me to give him another chance."

Erica shakes her head. "Hell, no. I can go with you if you want, but that won't be happening. You're reclaiming yourself and he gets no part of that."

"I mean, that's kind of why I'm doing this whole list thing. Because of him."

"Wait, what list? Why don't I know about this list?"

"My anti-boring list. Things that I wanted to do but Duncan never approved of them."

"What kind of things?" Erica asks.

"New things," I say. "Zip-lining. Pole dancing. Opening my own jewelry business. Going to a sex club."

Erica's jaw drops. Clearly me telling everyone I want to go to a sex club elicits the same response. "A sex club, babe? Fill me in."

I drop my head into my hands. "Ugh. Duncan always shot down anything I wanted to do and then he has the gall to call *me* boring. So I want to do all the things that I never got to do with him."

"And a sex club was on that list?"

"What's wrong with wanting to go to a sex club?" I peek at her between my fingers.

"Nothing. It's just not something I thought you would want to do."

"Well, I do. Because I am not the boring, Goody Two-shoes that Duncan thinks I am."

She throws her hands up in defense. "I didn't say you were. But if you want to go, I know a place."

Now I'm shocked. "Wait, really?"

She nods. "Yeah. Devon wanted to spice things up a few months ago so we tried it out. We had a good time."

"Why didn't I know about this?"

"Not something that I bring up in normal conversation." Erica eyes me. "But if you want to go, I'll take you."

"Yes. I do."

A sly grin slides across her face. "Then you meet with Duncan and hash it out with him and I'll take you to the sex club after."

"You're getting off easy."

Erica grins at me. "Wait until we hit the club."

Chapter Ten

CHLOE

DAX

When are you meeting Duncan?

CHLOE

In an hour

Leaving soon

You sure you don't want me to go with you?

I'll be fine

Besides, I don't want you punching your brother in the face

He deserves it

Not debating that

But it's time I had a conversation with him like an adult

Think he'll be able to do that?

Well, if he can't, end of conversation

Goodbye

The end

Never have to see that scumbag again

Call me after and let me know how it goes

I will

And if I'm not allowed to punch Duncan,
you can't either

<<how rude gif>>

Hey, you gotta protect those hands if you
want to start your business

I hate when you make sense

One of us has to be calm and collected
when it comes to my brother

No punching. Got it

Call you later

Good luck

God, I wish my foot would quit shaking. The longer I sit here at this tiny little coffee shop waiting for Duncan, the more nervous I get.

Maybe I should have had Dax come as a buffer, but I know that would only piss Duncan off more. And if we're going to have a conversation between the two of us, I need it to be a one and done.

Because it's not something I want to have to do again.

Glancing at my watch, I shouldn't be surprised that Duncan is late. He said to meet him at three, so I was here a few minutes early. Maybe he thinks it's a power move to show up late, but I really don't care. I just want this to be over.

As the minutes tick by, the nerves settle and the annoyance grows. This is just like Duncan to be late. He never had any sense of urgency to be anywhere on time. It was one of my biggest pet peeves about him. Something I overlooked when I agreed to marry him.

Another reason I'm glad to be done with him.

Before I can pull my phone out and call him, he waltzes in through the front door. His hair is slicked back and a dark pair of sunglasses covers his eyes. A tight black T-shirt shows off his biceps as khaki shorts cling to his thighs.

Ugh. I can't believe I was ever into him.

Pulling off his sunglasses, he looks around the coffee shop. A smile is firmly in place until he locks eyes with me in the corner.

It softens, like he's trying to butter me up.

There will be no buttering me up, Duncan. Save your butter for someone else.

"Chloe. Baby. It's so good to see you. I've missed you."

He goes in for a kiss, but I turn away. There is no way in hell I am going to let him convince me to get back with him.

"Duncan. You wanted to meet," I state, matter-of-factly.

I cross my arms and lean back in the chair. Tension and coffee perfume the air around us.

He tucks his sunglasses into the collar of his shirt and shoves a hand through his brown hair.

"You don't miss me?" He aims another smile my direction. "It's been months since we've seen each other."

Nothing. I feel nothing but anger and bitterness toward this man.

"And whose fault is that?" I quirk a brow at him.

"You're the one that ran out on our wedding, baby. Not me."

"Don't baby me," I hiss. "You're the one that was cheating *on me.*"

"Who says I was cheating?"

He looks relaxed. At ease. Like he doesn't have a care in the world.

What an asshole.

I hate that I let myself get so taken by him.

"I heard you talking to your side piece on the phone, Duncan. You really couldn't keep it in your pants for a few hours?"

Although, it got me out of marrying him, so can I really complain now?

"You don't know what you heard." Duncan leans over the table, stabbing his finger against the mosaic surface. "You heard one part of a conversation that wasn't meant for you."

I roll my eyes. "I wasn't supposed to hear you on the phone with your girlfriend? I'm *so* sorry."

"Look, I'm trying to make peace here, Chloe. I am ready to take you back and marry you because I can be the bigger person."

"Bigger person?" My skin is boiling I'm so mad.

He wants to be the bigger person? When he is the one that was cheating on me? Hell, no.

"Then tell me the truth."

Duncan looks confused. "What truth?"

"That you were cheating on me."

His dark brown eyes study me. As if he's trying to see what he can get away with telling me.

I don't know what fantasy world he lives in, but if he thinks he can lie again and get away with it, he's lost it.

Duncan takes my hand and I rip it away from him, trying not to let my blood curdle at his touch.

"There was only ever you, baby."

"Unbelievable!" I scoff, throwing my hands up in the air, drawing the stares of people around us. "You can't even tell the truth now. Was this how our marriage was going to be? Me, waiting at home for you, while you ran around with your tramp?"

"Grow up, Chloe. She's not a tramp."

"Oh, so there is a she now." I cluck my tongue, shaking my head. "Finally owning up to it."

"What's your problem, Chloe? Everyone cheats on everyone these days. Who the fuck cares?"

"Who the fuck cares?" My voice sounds shrill to my own ears. Now I'm fuming. If smoke were to come out of my ears, I wouldn't be surprised. "Silly me for thinking I'd want my husband to stay loyal to me."

"Then why don't you marry Dax?" Duncan bites out. "If you want someone to wait on you hand and foot, marry him."

"What?" That shocks me into silence.

"You heard me. Dax is the perfect man who can do no wrong." Bitterness oozes from his voice. "I'm tired of being compared to him."

"Who compared you to Dax?"

"You always did."

"I never did. You are your own person, Duncan, and you're responsible for your own actions."

"Whatever."

"I don't know what I ever saw in you."

"Then go be with my brother."

I slap my hands on the table between us. "Why do you keep saying that? Are you jealous of him?"

I was always careful around Duncan to make sure I never brought Dax up too much. I didn't want to get in the middle of the two of them, but leave it to Duncan to make it an issue.

"Why would I be jealous of him?"

"You sound like it to me."

"Probably never even had sex before," Duncan whispers.

"You're just being mean." I grab my purse and stand up. "We're done."

Duncan pulls his sunglasses from his shirt. "So that's a no then?"

"The fact that you can ask me that with a straight face tells me everything I need to know, Duncan. It's a hell no. If you were the last man on the planet, I wouldn't say yes to you for anything."

"Fine." He stands, a solid foot and a half taller than I am. "I want my ring back."

"No way. You don't get to act like the wronged party here. Go cry to your girlfriend. Or your side piece. I don't really care anymore."

"And here I thought we could have an adult conversation." Duncan shakes his head.

"If you could tell the truth, we would."

"I told you the truth, Chloe. You're the one that doesn't want to accept it."

"Fuck you, Duncan. I hope you get an STD and your dick falls off."

And on those parting words, I storm out of the coffee shop.

Was it the most adult of responses? No.

But damn, did that feel good.

Chapter Eleven

DAX

Another cryptic text from Chloe.

Throughout our entire friendship, I don't think I've ever gotten as many texts like this as I have since her wedding.

At least this time I'm meeting her someplace outside of the city. Which tells me that her meeting with Duncan didn't go well.

Pulling into a dirt parking lot, I throw my truck in park and hop out.

Nashville's Zip-lining Adventures is painted in red on a wooden sign. People mill about as I walk up to a small shack.

"Can I help you?" an older man sitting behind the counter asks.

"I'm looking for someone."

"Chloe?" he questions.

"Yes."

He points behind him. "She's getting in her harness. Told us to be on the lookout for a confused guy. You seem to fit the bill."

"Thanks."

At least I'm predictable. I find the sidewalk behind the building leading to a row of people stepping into gear. The familiar blonde at the front draws my attention.

"You're here," she says once she spots me.

"And what exactly is here?"

"I figured it was time to tackle another item from my list."

A man is adjusting the straps on her harness as she tells me this. A soft breeze blows through the tops of the trees.

"I take it meeting Duncan didn't go well?"

Chloe pierces me with a look that tells me all I need to know. "Not at all."

"And instead of talking through it with me, you decided to go zip-lining?" I look around. A family is walking toward one of the tall platforms. Others appear to be returning from their trip.

"Nothing a little adrenaline boost can't fix."

"You going with her?" the guy helping Chloe asks me.

"He is."

"I am?" I question.

Chloe nods. "Yes. I already paid for you. We're doing it together."

"Jesus," I mutter, scrubbing my hand over the back of my neck.

This is not how I imagined my afternoon going. After a good practice with the team, I was ready to grill out and have an easy night in.

Zip-lining was not on the agenda. It's not something I ever wanted to do, but for Chloe, I can't say no.

"I'll help you get fitted for a safety harness and go over everything with you."

"Great."

The attendant finds the right size harness for me and starts hooking me in.

"This is going to be fun." Chloe is grinning from ear to ear under her helmet.

"Are we going to talk about what happened with Duncan?" I ask.

Chloe might be excited, but I'm nervous. Heights? Never been my thing. I prefer to keep my feet on the ground and my skates on the ice.

She shrugs. "Do we have to right now?"

"If you're making me go zip-lining, then yes. I don't like heights."

"You don't? How do I not know this?" Chloe asks. She waves me off. "You don't have to go."

"Because I always thought you didn't like heights, so it never came up."

"I don't, but this isn't that high up," Chloe says.

"About thirty feet or three stories," the guy confirms. "Not bad at all."

"He doesn't have to go," Chloe says. "I can do it by myself."

"I'm not chickening out now. Not if we're doing it together."

"You sure?"

I nod. "I'm sure. Let's go."

Chloe grabs my hand and gives it a squeeze, but I don't let her let go. I need something to hold on to so my nerves don't get the best of me.

This is one of those things that I always kept to myself. Mainly because Duncan was the one who pushed me off a high bluff into a river when we were in high school. I've hated heights ever since.

Probably about the same time my feelings toward my own brother changed.

I listen intently as we get the safety speech. The fact that it's not the longest course here is my saving grace.

Thank fuck for that.

"Since you're bigger, we'll put you in back and clip your girl in front of you," the attendant says.

"Thanks," Chloe answers before I can correct him.

Your girl.

God, I wish Chloe was my girl. I still don't know what happened with my brother, but I can't imagine it was good if we ended up here.

"Once you're ready, you'll push off from this platform and keep your legs up as you go into the next. My colleague will help you at the next spot. Any questions?"

I shake my head at the man as he starts to attach Chloe in front of me.

It feels too good. *She* feels too good trapped between my legs as the carabiner is secured. Every scared and anxious thought at doing this goes out of my mind as the guy has me wrap my arms around Chloe as she takes hold of the contraption holding us to the line.

Yup. This was a really bad idea. Holding Chloe like this is bringing all sorts of reactions out in me. Namely, my dick.

Get a grip.

This is not the time or place to be having these kinds of feelings for Chloe. But it's hard to ignore how soft and pliable her body is in my arms. I've never let myself go there and I'm doing it now?

"You ready?"

"Yes," I answer, not even thinking.

The faster we get done, the faster I can put this problem behind me.

We step off the platform and my stomach drops as we

fly down the line. Chloe's shouts echo in my ears as I tighten my grip on her.

"Fuck!" I shout.

The sun flashes through the tops of the trees as we speed toward the second platform, kicking our feet onto the landing pad.

"Holy shit!" Chloe squeals as we get untethered from one line to the next. "I can't believe we did that."

Her face is full of excitement.

"Not as bad as I thought."

She smacks me in the chest. "Could have fooled me."

"The first one is always the hardest." The guy on the platform moves us into place as another couple takes off in front of us. This platform is bigger, with a few more people in front of us to go. "The next ones are shorter and get progressively closer to the ground. Nothing to worry about."

Chloe flits her gaze to mine. Those damn blue eyes of hers that I can never say no to. "See? It'll get better."

"It really wasn't that bad."

She pecks me on the cheek, not helping my earlier problem. "I know you didn't want to come, but I'm glad you did."

"Care to tell me what happened with Duncan?"

This close to her, I can feel the fury coming off of her. "He still wanted to get back together. Acted like it would be so magnanimous of him to take me. All I wanted was for him to admit he was cheating on me and he couldn't even do that. Until he said no one is loyal."

"He seriously said all that?"

She nods. "Yup. Said if I wanted someone loyal, I should go after you."

"Why was he bringing me into it?"

"I don't know. Jealous maybe?"

"Jealous of me? Never."

We move forward, hooking ourselves in again. The time for conversation is over as we take off again.

But this time, my brother's words ring in my head.

Why on earth would he tell Chloe to be with me? He couldn't have meant it. He must have meant someone like me.

That's all. No need to spin out about it.

It at least helps distract me as we fly through the trees. Each zip line gets easier as we get closer to the ground. By the time we're heading toward the last one, I'm actually enjoying myself.

Maybe I could use an anti-boring list to get out of my rut too.

"I can't believe I've never done that before," Chloe says as we descend down the stairs on the last platform, having finished the course. "That was so much fun."

"I don't know about *so much* fun, but I enjoyed it." I unclip my helmet as we walk back to the equipment return booth.

"Only because you were with me."

"Something like that." I smile at her.

With the uneven ground below us, she's eye to eye with me. Her blue eyes are happy. I like that I can make her feel better after having to deal with my brother.

"I'm sorry it didn't go better with Duncan this afternoon."

"I don't know what I was expecting. But at least I'm done and can put him behind me."

"Good. You deserve to be happy."

"I'm happy with you, Dax." Chloe smiles at me and I hate the way my traitorous body reacts. "Thank you."

"For what?"

"For doing this with me even though you were scared."

She pecks me on the cheek before hugging me. "You're the best friend I've ever had."

"You know I'm always here for you."

No matter how much it hurts that I can't have you the way I want.

"C'mon. I'll buy you dinner to celebrate both of us doing things we normally wouldn't do."

"I'll buy. You've had enough excitement for one day."

"Deal." She squeezes me close before letting go. "But I'm going to make you dinner next week before your first preseason game."

"It's hard to believe the season is almost here already," I say.

"That's because you guys went far last season. Hopefully, next year you'll go even further."

"God, I hope so."

"Me too. Because I want to be there cheering you on when you do win."

I wink at her. "I'll make sure of that."

There is no one else I want more at my side *when* we lift the cup. Only Chloe. She's the most important person in my life.

Even if we'll only ever be *just friends.*

Chapter Twelve

CHLOE

I don't know why everything has to be perfect tonight, but it has to be *perfect.* I check the oven one more time to make sure the lasagna is cooking at the right temperature. The salads are ready and perfectly dressed. All that needs to go in is the garlic bread in a few minutes.

I sip on wine, cooling my simmering nerves. Why am I nervous having Dax over for dinner? He's my best friend. I wanted to do something for him after everything he's done for me this summer. Especially after he went zip-lining with me when he hates heights.

It's weird how you can learn something new about your best friend after you've known them for more than half your life. But zip-lining with Dax? It was the most fun I've had in a long time. Everything lately has felt heavy. Weighted.

That day was fun. I haven't laughed so much…since I can't remember when.

Maybe a little too much fun. Because I enjoyed being in Dax's arms. It's a thought I've had to shake several times this past week while I've been working. I enjoyed the feel of his fingers digging into my sides. The way his thighs wrapped around me.

Nope. Not going there. Not at all.

I push the thoughts away.

Dax is my best friend. Hell, I ran away from his brother. It's not like the two of us could ever be together.

There's a knock at my door and I smile.

Right on time. Just like he always is. Setting my drink down on the counter, I cross the short distance to answer it.

And wow.

Dax is wearing a pair of jeans and a short-sleeved, black patterned button-down shirt that clings to his biceps. It's subtly sexy.

Wait, *what?*

I've never had that thought about Dax in my life.

Dax is sexy? I can't be thinking that. I'm not allowed to think Dax is sexy. He's off-limits. He's my ex-fiancé's brother.

He is in the no-go zone.

"Are you going to let me in?"

"Hi. Sorry." I shake myself out of my stupor and open the door for him.

He passes by in a whiff of soap and fresh laundry detergent.

"These are for you."

He pulls a bouquet of daisies out from behind his back.

"You know, you didn't have to bring me anything. This was a thank you for you." A dopey grin spreads across my face.

He gives me that charming smile of his, the easy grin that helps set anyone at ease.

"I can never come empty-handed. Besides, you could use some flowers around here."

"Are you saying my place is drab?"

I take the bouquet and head into the kitchen. Seeing as how I have no vases—not enough room to store them—I grab one of my Knights cups and fill it with water.

"No. I know you like daisies, so I wanted to bring you some."

"Thanks, Dax." I set them on the counter. "They look great."

"And it smells even better in here."

"I hope lasagna is good for you. I have that, salad, and garlic bread."

He grins at me, rubbing his hands together with an excited look on his face. "Perfect meal before the season starts."

"Want a drink?" I ask, grabbing a glass.

"Sure. I'll have what you're having."

"Are you excited for the start of the season?" I pour him a glass and pass it over.

"It feels like just yesterday…"

"That you were out of the playoffs and I was running out on my wedding?"

"We're at the point of joking about it now?" he asks, taking a sip.

"I would say yes. I'm sixty percent past it at this point."

"I'm glad you can move on because I'll only worry about you during forty percent of the season, Sunshine."

"Why are you going to worry about me?"

I pull the garlic bread out of the freezer and pop it onto a tray. Taking the lasagna out to let it cool, I put the bread in the oven.

"I was worried about you getting back on your feet this summer." Dax looks around.

"I couldn't have done it without you." I walk around the counter. "Do you want to see what I've been working on this week?"

"Show me."

A small, velvet tray sits on the coffee table in the living room. There are only four rings, but they are perfect. All made of silver, a different colored gemstone sits on the tops in various shapes.

"It took me a while to figure out how to get the gems to stay, but I like how they turned out."

Dax studies them, picking each one up and rubbing his finger over the metal. "These are really good, Chloe. You've done a great job."

"You mean that?"

He nods. "You know I've always liked what you make."

"I know you do."

The silver of his necklace glints in the light.

"I don't know how long these took you to make, but I'm proud of you."

Dax turns his sweet brown eyes on me and passes the ring over. I suck in a breath as his fingers brush against mine.

It's the softest, briefest of touches. But it sets off a torrent of emotions inside of me. It sends me right back to the moment in his arms when we were zip-lining. How good it felt. If he hadn't come with me, I wouldn't be sitting here thinking about how much I want to feel his hands in other places.

Stop. It.

Dax is your best friend. You don't want to mess things up with him.

"Have you started selling them online?" Dax asks, breaking me out of my thoughts.

"One ring at a time."

"Do you think you'll venture outside of rings?"

I laugh. "Eventually. I need to get rings down first and maybe make more than two a day."

The oven timer dings and we head back into the kitchen. "How can I help?"

"Want to grab the salads and take them over to the table?"

"Sure."

My eyes watch Dax as he gets everything sorted on the card table. I tried to dress it up, but I didn't have much to use aside from throwing a floral tea towel over it.

As I scoop out two steaming pieces of lasagna onto our plates, my eyes track Dax. He's so at ease here. I've never noticed how efficiently or smoothly he moves in my space.

I like having him here. With the season getting ready to start, my time with him is going to be cut in half.

"Thanks for making dinner," Dax says as we both sit down.

"Here's to a great season." I hold up my glass in cheers and we clink. "I'm going to miss you once the season starts."

"You'll be too busy building your empire to miss me. You'll be all *Dax who?*"

The corner of his mouth quirks up in an easy smile before he digs into his dinner.

Butterflies flutter low in my belly.

Okay, that is new. I have never reacted this way to Dax. He's always been able to put me at ease.

"Me? Please. You'll be too busy being the best player on the ice."

"I like that you think that, Sunshine, but I don't think I will be. There are a lot of players better than I am."

"You're too humble," I say, cutting off a small bite of the casserole and savoring the garlic and tomato flavors.

"Honest. But I'm trying to improve."

"You're my favorite player if that means anything."

He smiles, starting the butterflies again. "You're biased."

"Biased or not, the Knights are lucky to have you."

"Let's not talk about me. What's next on your list you want to accomplish?"

I don't know why, but I don't want to talk about the *next* thing. The sex club. It feels weird now. I bypass it entirely.

"I'm thinking of roller derby next. Maybe writing a poem."

"Want me to try my hand at composing a poem right now?" Dax laughs.

"Think you can do it?" I set my fork down and lean back in my rickety chair.

"I remember how to write haiku."

"Go for it."

He looks around with an inquisitive look on his face before it lights up as it lands on me.

"This lasagna rules. The salad's really good too. I love garlic bread."

"Oh my God." I choke on my laughter. "Dax. I can't."

"That was solid gold. It would break the world record on your list for best haiku ever written."

I pat his hand. "Whatever you say, Dax."

"You write me one then."

"I do not write poems on demand." I point a finger at him. "If I'm going to write something, I need time."

"You're worried it's not going to live up to mine. It's okay to admit it, Chloe."

"Maybe I'll write one about the Knights."

Dax points his fork at me. "That one will take you time to perfect."

"I'll hit you with it when you least expect."

We spend the rest of dinner talking about the upcoming season and how to expand my business. This is what I love about Dax. He doesn't tell me what I want to hear, but helps me with different ideas that can help. I've watched him play since we became friends, so I know some about the game, but mostly it's me encouraging him. Sometimes as friends, that's all we can do.

That and sending him home with leftovers so I know he's fed.

"Are you sure you don't want to keep these?"

I push the Tupperware dish into his hands. "Positive. I can't eat all of that. I made it for you."

"Thanks, Chloe." He grabs the doorknob, ready to leave.

"See you later, Dax."

I watch him walk to his car, not wanting him to go. I want to call him back and have him stay. Create silly poems with him. Talk jewelry and business. Nothing and everything.

As he pulls away and I close the door to my small apartment, it feels too big. Too quiet. Like it needs someone else in here with me.

Not someone.

Dax.

Chapter Thirteen

DAX

CHLOE

Good luck this afternoon!

DAX

Thanks

But it's only preseason

I still want you to do well

I'm sorry I won't see you after the game

Why won't I see you after the game

Umm...

I mean, it's fine if you don't stay after

It's not a big deal

Well, Erica and I have plans

What are you doing?

Do you want me to tell you?

Now I have to know 😏

We're going to a sex club

Oh

Erica knows a place

Cool cool cool cool cool

Are you okay?

I don't think I've ever heard you say that
many cools at once

I'm cool

I mean good

Totally fine

You definitely don't sound it

Can you sound like something over text?

I know you

So I can tell

I'm totally cool

I figured this list item would be easier to do
with Erica

Sure

I get it

Totally fine with it

I might have to make a drinking game out
of you saying cool or fine

Don't

Breakaway

You need to keep it together if you're going
to a sex club

And you know, do sex things

I'll be fine

You're going to have to text me when you
get there and when you leave

Hourly updates too

Someone has to keep track of you

That's why I'm going with Erica

Devon is coming too

Is that her boyfriend?

Yeah

We'll be good

You know you don't have to do this if you
don't want to

I know

Just making sure

I'm good

You go worry about winning your game

Not worried at all, Sunshine

We've got it in the bag

I'll be cheering you on from the stands

Thanks

"Dax. Are you paying attention?"

"What?" My attention snaps to Marcus. "Yeah."

"Then what did he just say?" Noah asks.

"Don't be a dick," I fire back.

"What's got you so distracted?"

I clear my throat. "Focused on the game."

I don't need to tell the guys about Chloe's plans. Even though it's all I've been thinking about since she told me.

Hockey will be a good distraction. A distraction from thinking about what Chloe is planning on doing at the sex club.

"Dude. You really are distracted." Bode whacks me on the arm.

"It's the first game of the season. Give him a break," Jasper defends.

"Thank you. Just trying to get my head in the game," I say.

I push all thoughts of Chloe out of my mind and look ahead to our first opponent. Even though it's preseason, it's the first chance to see how all of us gel as a team on the ice. We've been practicing well together, but playing Seattle is going to be good for us.

They're one of the stronger teams in the league this season. Coach Andrews has done a good job of preparing us for them.

I've been pushing myself harder than ever. I want to be the best player I can be this season. I mean, I do every year, but having gotten so close to the finals and missing out, I want to do everything I can to help get us there.

Not to mention it'd be nice to be better than my brother.

"Alright, men, listen up." Coach Andrews calls our attention to him. "I know it's only a preseason game, but this afternoon I want to see everything we've been working on in practice. We're looking really good right now, and I'm excited to see how we put it all together for the game."

Looking around, a thrum of excitement simmers in the locker room. Guys are nodding their heads and others bump fists with the guy next to them.

"Let's have a good clean game and bring home a win!" Coach yells.

"Hell yeah!" Bode says next to me, bumping shoulders with me as we all start to file out of the locker room.

This is what I love. That energy before a game. The excitement is palpable. It's a fresh slate. No wins and no losses. Everyone is on an even playing field.

Taking the ice, we hear the crowd erupt.

This is the best feeling as we're cheered on by our fans as pregame festivities carry on around us. Before I know it, the anthems are over and the puck is dropping.

I take my place on the bench as the action starts. Maybe one of these days I'll be on the first line. I've been working hard to get there, so we'll see.

Marcus passes the puck over to Bode—whose stick work is impressive—as he moves down the ice. Between the two of them, they're lightning out there.

The two of them have only gotten better the longer they've been playing together. I love having players like them on our team because they make everyone around them elevate their game, which is something I'm trying really hard to do.

Before they can score, we change out the lines and I'm on the ice.

Everything fades away around me as the only thing that matters is the stick in my hand and the puck on the ice.

Heading into their zone, I'm ready as our winger sends

the puck to me. Seattle's defensemen are good as they stop us from setting up our play. Chasing them down, it's a battle to keep the puck out of the net.

It's a game of back-and-forth for the first two periods. By the third period, Marcus has managed to score before our first line is pulled to rest as the other lines take the ice. Even though it's only preseason, these guys are still fighting hard to show they're an asset to the team.

Seattle pulls their goalie at the end of the game, but to no avail. One of our guys is able to score on the empty net, earning us a 2-0 victory.

"Not a bad start to preseason," Jasper says, the two of us heading into the tunnel after shaking hands with the other team.

"Felt good to get back out there."

The two of us are some of the last guys in the locker room as the press is already hanging around, asking questions.

One of my least favorite parts of the job.

"Dax. You looked good out there tonight. How'd it feel to be back on the ice?" a reporter from one of the local networks asks.

"Great. It's always around this time I start to get antsy and want to get back to doing what I love."

He smiles back at me. "How was it watching Marcus and Bode out there tonight? They were on fire."

"They work well together on the ice. It's going to be a fun season watching them play together."

"Speaking of watching others play. You've been playing in your brother's shadow for a long time. With him looking to rejoin the league, are you worried about his play affecting yours?"

Only years of media training prevents me from rolling my eyes and wanting to curse this guy out. Except that's not who I am. Duncan? Yes. Me? I'm the calm, cool, and collected brother.

"I know any team would be lucky to have Duncan play for them." Seriously, thank God for that training because I don't know if I would be able to keep a straight face otherwise. "I'm going to continue to play my game the best that I can, and hopefully that will help the Knights win games."

"Thanks, Dax. Good luck this season."

"Thanks."

As the media clears out of the locker room, I hit the showers. I let the warm water sluice over my body. It felt good to get my legs under me as the season starts.

I can't wait to celebrate later with Chloe.

Oh, shit.

I can't.

I guess the game was a good distraction because I completely forgot where she's going tonight. I know she's with Erica and will be safe with her, but now that gnawing feeling is back.

Like I shouldn't be letting her go—but she's an adult and can make her own decisions. I shouldn't let my worries of her being unsafe or uncomfortable there get in the way of her doing what she wants.

That's the whole point of that damn list. To do things that Duncan wouldn't.

Does that make me like Duncan?

It's not that I'm *not* supporting her, but she didn't ask me to go with her.

Damn it. I don't know why I'm so torn up about this. Shutting off the shower, I grab my towel and head back into the locker room.

"You want to grab a drink tonight? The rest of the guys are busy," Jasper says. He's buttoning up his shirt before grabbing his jacket.

"Sorry, I can't. I have plans with Chloe."

I make up my mind in that minute. I don't care if Chloe sees me or not, but I'll feel better knowing I am there.

"Even you have someone," he bemoans.

"Sorry?" I question. "I mean, it's not like Chloe and I are dating."

"Yeah, but you're still hanging out with her."

"Get yourself a best friend then."

"Like a dog?" Jasper looks at me like I'm an idiot. "I don't need a dog."

"I meant a person, but maybe a cat would work out nicely for you."

"You're not the first person to tell me that."

"Who else is telling you that you need a cat?" I ask, grabbing my boxers to pull on.

"Doesn't matter. I'll consider it since all you guys are ditching me."

"We're not ditching you." I drop the towel and grab my shirt. "Different priorities right now. You'll find someone."

"Have fun with Chloe." Jasper claps me on the shoulder and heads out. The rest of the guys wave goodbye as I finish getting dressed.

I don't have the first idea of where Chloe is tonight. There can't be that many sex clubs around Nashville, right?

If I'm going to do this, I can't look like myself. Thank God we had an afternoon game, because I need to make a stop before going.

And I know just the place.

Chapter Fourteen

CHLOE

I can't believe I'm doing this. Of all the things on my list, I thought this one would be the last one I would do.

Turns out, it wasn't. With not much time to get ready after the game, I shimmy into my tiniest dress and swipe on one last coat of lip gloss.

ERICA

Downstairs

Ready when you are!

CHLOE

Two more minutes and I'll be down

FLUFFING MY HAIR out one more time, I give myself a once-over in the mirror.

Hair curled? Sprayed to an inch of its life.

Makeup? Immaculate.

Sexy black dress? A must.

Stepping into my red heels, I grab my clutch and head out, locking the door behind me.

"Damn, girl. You look hot!" Erica yells from the car.

"Thanks."

I hop into the backseat, adjusting my skirt.

"Erica says you've never been to one of these places?" Devon asks, turning out of the parking lot.

"Not yet."

"Erica and I can show you the ropes. And if you want to leave, we can," he says. "They're all about safety at this place, so you're in good hands."

"Thanks. Erika already filled me in as to what I should expect."

The lights glimmer ahead of us as we cross the bridge into the city. Each mile we travel ratchets up my nerves. This is the most un-Chloe-like thing I've ever done. Probably will ever do.

I need to prove to myself that I can do this.

Driving away from the more popular bar scene, Devon leads us to a quiet downtown street before parking. It's the most nondescript building. A bouncer is standing outside a black door, lit overhead from the streetlamps.

Music from a nearby bar filters over as the sun starts to sink closer to the horizon.

"You ready?" Erica asks, looking as good as ever in a green dress that shows off her curves.

"I'm ready." I take a deep breath, smoothing my hand over my own outfit.

"You can back out if you want to."

"I'm not."

Steeling my spine, I follow Erica inside after flashing our IDs to security. The room is dimly lit, with walls covered in thick velvet drapes. A sexy woman with her hair in a tight bun and red lipstick is standing behind the counter, tapping away on a tablet.

"How can I help you this evening?" Even her voice is sultry.

"There'll be three of us tonight," Devon says.

"Please sign these release forms. You must agree to everything on the forms before you'll be allowed entry." She passes over three clipboards. "Read carefully and ask if you have any questions."

It only takes a few minutes to read through everything and sign off. Instead of scaring me off, it makes me excited.

I can't believe I'm doing this.

"Enjoy your evening." The woman nods to us as we're shown into the main room.

And wow. It's nothing like I thought it would be.

More of the same heavy, velvet drapes curtain the walls. A bar is off to one side with people chatting and ordering drinks. Others are spread around chairs and tables that line the walls. A few people are making out in one corner, but that's it.

"Not quite what you thought, right?" Erica nudges me in the side.

"Not at all."

"You want to grab a drink with us and feel the place out?"

I shake my head. "I'll get a glass of wine, but I think I want to sit and take it all in."

Erica leans in, pecking me on the cheek. "Make sure to have *some* fun."

"I will."

Devon orders our drinks as my eyes scan the crowd. I expected to walk into a mass orgy. Turns out I was wrong.

Very wrong.

Drinks are passed over and I watch as Erica and Devon take off in the opposite direction of where I head.

I can't get far because a familiar face stops me in my tracks. Well, a mostly familiar face.

"Dax?" I whisper hiss.

"No."

"What?"

Confused, I drop down onto the free seat next to him.

"My name is Drake." A fake mustache—that looks more like a caterpillar on his upper lip—twitches.

"Drake?" I snort laugh.

"It's nice to meet you…" he trails off, extending his hand.

This is how we're going to play it?

"Cora." I smile, taking his hand. "Can I ask why you're here tonight, *Drake?*"

"Well, someone I know was going to be here so I wanted to make sure they were okay."

"I think they are." I sip on my drink.

Dax—or Drake, as I should call him—sips on a dark, brown liquor.

"Much different than I thought it would be."

"Right?" I rest my hand on his thigh without thinking about it. "I didn't think this is what it would be like."

"Way more sex?"

"Yes." I nod. "Does it make you feel better about your *friend?*"

"It does. It's obvious she doesn't need me here, so I can probably go."

"No," I blurt out, grabbing on to his forearm. "I want you to stay. I mean, stay for your friend."

"Okay."

Dax links his hand with mine. An electricity I've never felt spreads through me. I don't think I've ever noticed—or let myself notice—just how soft his hands are. Dark brown eyes lock onto mine, swimming with emotion.

Is it getting hot in here, or is it just me?

"Need anything to drink?"

I jump a foot, banging my knee against the table as a server checks in on us.

"I'll take another bourbon," Dax says. "I'd go ahead and get her another glass of wine."

"Thank you."

"You okay?" Dax asks, rubbing his fingers on my knee.

"Uh-huh."

I down the rest of my wine. I am so far from okay, it's not even funny. Dax and I have never shied away from touches. Hugs here and there. Kisses on the cheek. We've always been like that.

Why now is a touch from him making me crazy with need?

A part of me that I thought I hid away is coming back to life with each circle he rubs into my knee.

Lust.

Desire.

Wanton need for my best friend.

"You sure?" he asks as fresh drinks are dropped off.

"I guess I was jumpy before I came in here."

"Do you want to go?" he asks.

"I promise, I'm okay."

I settle back into the seat as Dax pulls his hand off my knee. That'll help. That and more wine.

"I honestly thought there'd be a lot more sex happening."

"I thought so too. Guess I really had no idea what I was signing up for."

"Makes me feel like I was overreacting."

I nudge his shoulder with mine. "I'm glad you're here."

"Me too."

A couple takes the empty seats across from us and immediately start making out. His hand snakes under her skirt as his other hand maneuvers her top down. The two of them don't have a care in the world as things escalate.

Not wanting to be caught staring, my eyes track over the room. It's like a switch flipped and more people are making out and fooling around than before.

It's…well, it's downright hot to see.

"Wow," I whisper.

"Do you—" Dax is cut off before he can get his question out.

"Hi."

A beefy man with a thick beard comes over to us, a drink in hand. Before I can get a word out, Dax is pulling me onto his lap. "She's taken."

"Sorry." He slinks away, not looking back.

Holy. Shit.

I have never felt so possessed by any one person in my entire life. Dax's fingers dig into my side, hot like an iron.

I feel it *everywhere*. Heat builds in my core. It's the most innocent of touches, but I want more. Am craving more.

With Dax.

"Sorry, if you want to—"

"No," I snap, cutting him off. "I'm fine here."

I want this feeling with Dax to continue. I want to bottle it up to revisit anytime I'm feeling…needy, downright hungry for my best friend.

Oh my God, I want Dax.

Based on the growing problem I'm feeling now, I can say he wants me too. It must be because of the sex club and everyone else getting off.

I wonder what it would feel like to be doing with Dax

what the others are doing with each other. Image after image flash through my mind.

Of being back in Dax's bedroom with him. Of his head between my legs, eating me out. Thrusting into me. How good he would make me feel.

"Oh God," I purr, wiggling my hips. It does nothing to help Dax.

"Fuck, Chloe," he bites out. "You really can't do that."

"Why not?" It slips out before I can stop it.

"Because…"

"Because why?"

"We can't."

Flipping around, I'm straddling Dax. A pained look is on his face as his strong hands drift down my thighs.

"Because you're my best friend?" I ask.

"Yeah."

"Cora doesn't know Drake though," I argue. "What if…"

"You really want to do this?"

I trace a finger over the fake mustache he's wearing. "I do if you do."

When he arches his hips into me, I can't help the groan that escapes as he pulls me close to him, lips ghosting my ear. "If we do this, nothing changes. Just a quick way to get off. No kissing or anything. This is Drake and Cora. Tomorrow, we'll go back to being Dax and Chloe."

"Nothing changes."

I swivel my hips over his cock. If this is all the two of us get—a quick dry-humping session in a sex club—I'm going to enjoy every second.

Dax kisses a warm path up and down my neck as I keep moving over his hard cock. We're reading each other perfectly, moving in sync. Nothing has ever felt so, so… right.

I sink my fingers through Dax's hair as he moves me over him. The soft cotton of his pants against my clit is pushing me closer and closer to the edge.

I want more, but this is all I'm going to get tonight. I don't know if we could do more and not have things change.

But this? Humping Dax right now? It's foreplay but so damn good.

"I'm getting close," I whisper, tossing my head back.

Dax tugs my earlobe between his teeth, commanding, "Look at me. I want to see your face when you come."

"Yes."

Inhibition is thrown out the window. I don't know this person who has taken over my body, but she is taking what she wants. And right now, I want this man to make me come.

Dax's hands slide over to my ass, moving me faster. Grinding me down harder. One more thrust of his hips up has me exploding.

"Dax!"

I don't care that we're supposed to be Drake and Cora. All common sense is gone as I let pleasure take over my body. The sparks. The heat. Everything.

Everything feels out of this world as the grunts and squeezes from Dax tell me he's come too. Breathing hard, I collapse into his arms.

He holds me close, rubbing circles into my back as we come down from our high. I don't think anything could top this.

"Take me home?" I ask.

"Of course," he says, helping me to my feet. I'm in a blurry haze as lust carries me away.

"Do you need to let Erica know?"

"Yeah." I nod, pulling out my phone and letting her

know who's taking me home. Because she would ask. I know she'll want more, but not right now.

Right now, I want to live in this post-orgasm bubble from Dax just a little longer.

It's dark by the time Dax helps me into his truck. He cracks the windows, letting a warm breeze flow through the cab of the truck.

I can't believe we did that together. I never thought anything like that would happen with Dax of all people. But I don't regret it for one minute.

The city flies by as Dax takes me to my place, pulling up in a parking spot and turning the engine off.

"You don't have to come up." I look over at him. There's a softness there that makes my heart pitter-patter. "It's okay."

"Chloe—"

"Cora can do it." I wink at him.

"Fine. I'm going to wait until you're inside. Flash your porch light at me so I know you're in safely, okay?"

"I can do that." I rest my arms on the open window. "Hey, Dax?"

"Yeah?"

"Thanks for tonight."

"Anything for you, Chloe."

"Bye."

He doesn't leave until I turn my light on in my apartment. Only then does he head home.

I'm left wishing he would take me with him and we could spend the rest of the night together.

But that would change everything.

And I won't let that happen.

Chapter Fifteen

DAX

DAX

I need help

BODE

It's seven in the morning

BODE

On a Saturday

BODE

Why are you texting us so early?

Is it that big of a deal?

BODE

I've been up for an hour with Caleb

BODE

He's screaming his head off because his molars are coming in

MARCUS

I don't miss those days

Can you guys help?

BODE

Why are you awake?

Because I couldn't sleep

MARCUS

You don't have kids

MARCUS

You should be sleeping for at least another
three hours

You're awake

MARCUS

I have kids

MARCUS

But they didn't wake me up

BODE

Gross

BODE

No one wants to hear about your sex life

MARCUS

I didn't say that was what I was doing

BODE

You implied it

MARCUS

Dax, why do you need our help?

NOAH

Why are all of you fuckers awake?

NOAH

I'm trying to sleep

JASPER

So go back to sleep

NOAH

I can't

NOAH

Too much buzzing

GRAHAM

And now I'm awake because Noah's awake

BODE

Okay, no sex talk today

NOAH

We were not having sex

GRAHAM

Unlike Marcus

MARCUS

I never actually said I was having sex

GRAHAM

What other reason would you be up?

BODE

Can we get back to Dax?

JASPER

I bet that fondue goes down pretty smooth
with some Swiss beer

GRAHAM

What in the world?

BODE

Why is Jasper texting nonsense?

NOAH

Because we're all awake at seven in the
morning

MARCUS

Ignore Jasper

MARCUS

Back to Dax

NOAH

Yeah, what's up?

Bode said no sex talk

BODE

Well now you have to tell us

Chloe and I had sex

MARCUS

Did you mean to type Chloe?

BODE

Your best friend Chloe?

NOAH

Wait, you two had sex?

GRAHAM

Like, Chloe Chloe? Your best friend?

JASPER

Oh shit

Oh shit is the appropriate response here

MARCUS

Can I ask what led up to you two
having sex?

NOAH

When a man and a woman like each
other...

MARCUS

You're a dick

GRAHAM

It's what you get when you wake him up
this early

BODE

This seems to have come out of the blue

BODE

I mean, we all know you love her, but it
escalated quickly

We went to a sex club together

JASPER

You, Dax Fletcher, went to a sex club?

NOAH

Is this some sort of April Fool's joke?

GRAHAM

It's September, babe

NOAH

But Dax went to a sex club

NOAH

Bode does

NOAH

Dax doesn't

BODE

Hey! I do not

MARCUS

I have to agree

MARCUS

This does seem weird

It was on Chloe's list

JASPER

What list?

Her list to prove she's not boring

MARCUS

And a sex club is the way to do that?

About the least boring thing people do

JASPER

You're right on that account

BODE

So what did you do at the sex club?

MARCUS

I think we know what they did

NOAH

Yeah, we're not questioning the fact that he and Chloe did it

Well...

BODE

Is this why you need help? Do we need to explain sex to you?

NOAH

We only assumed you've had it before

You guys suck

MARCUS

Don't be dicks

It was more like dry humping

BODE

Not going to lie, I do enjoy that

BODE

A lot

NOAH

Gross

MARCUS

Why are we talking about sex so early?

JASPER

Obviously Dax needs our help because he doesn't know how to deal with this

> Thank you!

> That's what I've been trying to get to this whole time

NOAH

Okay, so you and Chloe were dry humping

NOAH

I'm assuming because we're having this conversation you enjoyed it?

> Yes. We both did

BODE

So what's the problem?

> I knew I shouldn't have come to you guys with this

MARCUS

Too late to unpull that thread

GRAHAM

Yup, cat's out of the bag

GRAHAM

What are you going to do now?

> That's the part I don't know yet

BODE

Why are you talking to us about it?

JASPER

Because he needs to know how to talk to Chloe about it

Clearly a great choice on my part

One I'm regretting

BODE

Tell her you've been in love with her since dinosaurs roamed the earth and you want to be with her

MARCUS

Have an honest, adult conversation with her

JASPER

Tell me you're the oldest one in the group without telling me you're the oldest one in the group

MARCUS

Fuck off

MARCUS

I have the wisdom of years under my belt

NOAH

Is that what we're calling it?

So have an adult conversation

JASPER

The exact opposite of whatever this convo is

You make it sound so easy

NOAH

Telling someone you love them is never easy, but also the easiest thing at the same time

BODE

Who are you and what have you done with Noah?

GRAHAM

He has his moments

JASPER

Apparently right after he wakes up

BODE

Maybe we need to wake him up like this
more often

GRAHAM

Having been on the receiving end of waking
him up too early, please don't

I'm going to go plan what I'm going to say
to Chloe

BODE

We can always help you tonight

Tonight?

MARCUS

We leave for our road trip

Shit. I forgot

JASPER

How could you forget?

JASPER

You have to keep Bode in line

I don't have to keep him in line

BODE

I keep myself in line, thank you very much

GRAHAM

That sounds kind of dirty

NOAH

Okay, now that we've decided we can
discuss this tonight, I'm going back to bed

GRAHAM

I'll take this into the kitchen

NOAH

Can you bring me a cup of coffee?

BODE

Aren't you two right next to each other?

GRAHAM

Your point?

BODE

Why don't you just tell him without telling all of us?

NOAH

Punishment for waking me up

BODE

Go back to bed

NOAH

Believe me, I'm trying

I'll see you guys later tonight

JASPER

Don't think you're getting out of talking to us about this

I would never

BODE

Good. Because when Stevie wakes up, I'm going to get her input on how to broach the subject with Chloe

MARCUS

I'm asking Harper too

NOAH

Don't forget the sugar!

BODE

Seriously, you live in the same house

BODE

Go make your own coffee

NOAH

Blame Dax

Love you, too

BODE

That was easy!

BODE

Just say that to Chloe

JASPER

Really, Bode?

MARCUS

It's a wonder you won over Stevie

BODE

I have no problem telling her how much I love her

GRAHAM

Then you can help us tonight

BODE

Oh, I'm on it

BODE

We'll make sure Dax gets the girl

I can only hope

Chapter Sixteen

CHLOE

Everything changed.

We said nothing would change, and in the span of twelve hours, *everything* has changed. Why did I think getting off with Dax at the sex club would be a good idea? I wasn't thinking.

I was too wrapped up in getting the whole sex club experience to stop and think what it might do to our friendship.

I spent the entire night tossing and turning. Remembering what Dax looks like when he comes. His strong hands on my body. His grunts as he came.

Dax is no longer my best friend. How do you even quantify what we did together? I don't have the right words.

I have never thought about Dax like that. At least not since high school. I always liked him back then, but it was Duncan who asked me out first.

Ever since then, Dax has been firmly in the best friend zone.

Now? Now, I have no idea what zone he is in. It's

murky. Clouded. Is there a *my best friend and I got off together at a sex club and now I have feelings for him* zone?

Because if so, that's where I need to be.

I cannot stop remembering how good his hands felt on me as I was dry humping his dick like I'd never had sex before.

I cannot stop remembering how good his breath felt on my neck as he whispered words of encouragement in my ear. Something I'd never imagined before.

And I cannot stop remembering the feeling of us coming together. The way his fingers dug into my skin. How he held me close through my release.

Shit.

I really shouldn't be thinking about this right now because it's making me greedy for more.

But Dax and I said nothing would change. Having these thoughts about Dax—about wanting *more* with Dax—would change things.

It's not like I can talk to him about this. What if he's not feeling the same things as I am? What if he went to bed feeling completely normal about where the two of us stand? I mean, he's the one that said nothing changes.

But you can't come with your best friend and *not* have things change.

Instead, I pull up my texts and send one to Erica.

CHLOE

Dax and I had sex last night

IT'S STILL EARLY. She and Devon stayed later than we did,

so there's no way she's awake. But within thirty seconds, my phone is vibrating in my hand with her call.

I can't even get a word out before her voice fills my ear.

"You had sex with Dax?! I know you two went off together, but I thought he was just keeping an eye on you."

"We—"

"I mean, this is Dax. This is your ex's brother and your best friend. Why did you not tell me this happened last night when you left?"

"Are you—"

"I mean, this is huge, Chloe. Huge," she continues without letting me answer. "I've kind of suspected that Dax always had feelings for you, but to happen at a sex club? Wow."

"Wait. You think Dax has feelings for me?" I ask. Not where I was going to start the conversation, but it's the only thing I can think about now.

"You are the only person in the world that doesn't know he has been in love with you since the beginning of time."

"But I've been with Duncan."

"And? That doesn't make his feelings magically disappear."

"But…"

Dax has feelings for me? I thought that he went with me last night to help me with my list. Could he really have feelings for me?

The rose-colored glasses are off. Every single memory I have with Dax over the last few years comes rushing into focus. Well, a clearer focus now that Erica has blown the lid off something that seems so obvious now that she points it out.

Sure, we've talked about me dating him, but she never

mentioned him having feelings. I thought it was because he was there and convenient that she wanted me to date him.

"See what I mean?" she asks over the phone. "You're realizing what's always been in front of you."

"Wow."

Who knew one night at a sex club could change everything? Everyone but the two of us, apparently.

"More importantly, Chloe. How was the sex?"

"Erm…"

"You said you had sex. Did you not have sex, or do I need to go over the finer points with you of how to properly have sex?"

"We were dry humping." I clear my throat. "No kissing, because that would have made things messy, but God, do I ever want to kiss him."

"And you came?" she asks point blank. "I think that would make things more messy."

I snicker at her laugh.

"Yes. We both did."

"Damn, girl. You must be good to make a man like that come in his pants."

"What do you mean a man like that?" I ignore the other part of her statement.

"Do I really have to point out how sexy your best friend is? I mean, both of ours are." She laughs. "But Dax? He is hot. Not that powerful, overbearing kind of hot that Duncan is, you know?"

"Oh, I know." I roll my eyes.

"But Dax? Dax is that boy next door. The one you bring home to meet your parents and he's shy when you first introduce them. But when you bang? All bets are off."

"Tell me how you really feel."

"Look, Chloe. I know you've sworn off all men and hockey players, but Dax is different."

"I know he is."

"Duncan was the worst of all men combined. I mean, we've all been taken with a pretty face before, and it's not your fault he conned you into thinking he was a good guy. That would scare anyone off dating," she says.

"I'm scared of him hurting me," I confess, my voice getting quiet. "I don't think I would ever recover if Dax—"

"Sweetie," Erica cuts me off. "Dax would never hurt you. I don't think he would know how to. You're the earth and he's the moon, revolving around you."

"Isn't the sun supposed to be in there somewhere?" I laugh, easing the tension that builds in my chest.

"You're the sun, moon, and all the planets combined. You just have to decide whether you want to take the next step with Dax."

The next step. It seems so simple, but at the same time, also feels like a giant ravine.

Nerves are burbling up in my stomach. What if Dax doesn't want to take the next step? What if, after everything we did last night, he's fine with how things are and doesn't actually have feelings for me? I don't want to lose Dax, but it can't stay the same now.

Everything changed.

"Look, Chloe. I can feel you spinning out from here. Take a few days. Get lost in your jewelry and designs. Then, call Dax and talk to him. See how he's feeling."

I gasp. "You mean have a conversation like a grown-up?"

Erica laughs. "Yes. You're an adult and I know you can do it."

"Fine," I grumble. "Only because it's Dax and I don't think I can stew on this that long."

"If you make it two days, I'll be impressed."

"And for that reason, I'm going to take three."

"We'll see." She laughs. "Now, if you want to continue this conversation, I'm going to need some coffee."

"Go back to sleep. I'll be fine."

"Call me once you talk to Dax so I know how it goes."

"I will. Bye."

"Bye, babe."

I stare at my ceiling long after the call ends. Dax leaves for a short road trip this afternoon. I miss him when he's out of town, but this will give me the time to sort through the complicated mess of emotions swimming through me.

Erica is right about one thing. I need to have this conversation with Dax like a grown-up. I put off talking to Duncan for too long because I was mad and wanted him out of my life. That's the very last thing I want with Dax.

If only I can figure out how to start the conversation.

Hey, Dax. Remember that time we dry humped in a sex club and we said nothing would change?

Well, everything changed…

Chapter Seventeen

DAX

I'm doing it. I'm having the adult conversation.

I don't care that every single fiber of my being is stressed beyond belief. I was not this nervous before my first NHL game.

That was different.

This is different.

It's Chloe. My best friend. And I want to ask her to make this thing between us more permanent. We were lying to ourselves if we thought nothing could change. Everything changed. I'm hoping for the better, but that remains to be seen.

With the team's annual fundraiser gala coming up early in the season, I want to bring Chloe as my plus-one.

But I don't want to push my luck. It's been a hard few weeks for her. Why would she want to take a chance on me?

I'm hoping I might be able to convince her.

Packing up the last of the lunch items into the wicker basket, I grab the blue-and-white checkered blanket and head out to my truck.

I drop the basket into the backseat and pull out of the driveway. I know she said she was busy today since I had practice, but I'm hoping I can pull her away for at least an hour or two before I head over to the arena to start studying film.

I mean, everyone has to eat, right?

I smile, thinking about Chloe working on her dream. The one my brother never encouraged her to pursue.

My knuckles go white around the steering wheel. How did I get stuck with the world's biggest dick for a brother? Someone who treated his fiancée like utter shit?

Frankly, I'm glad she's done with him.

Chloe deserves better.

Flicking on my blinker, I turn into the parking lot of her apartment building and find an empty spot.

I spot her curtains from my seat, seeing her shadow move beyond. Even through the flimsy material, I can see just how sexy she is.

I only hope she says yes to me. But I won't know if I never get the courage to leave my truck.

Opening the truck door, I hop out and make the short walk to her apartment. Rapping my knuckles on her door, I wait.

When she greets me with a wide smile, I have to do everything in my power to keep it together. Because in a white tank top with a fancy lace pattern that covers her chest and a pair of cutoff jean shorts, she looks fucking stunning.

It's hard to be around her and not think of what the two of us have done together. Does she think about it as much as I do? It takes all I have to focus on hockey and not her every second of the day.

"Hey. What are you doing here?"

"I thought we could do lunch together today."

"Don't you have practice?"

"Not until later. I've got everything waiting in the truck."

"Umm." Chloe looks at the messy table behind her. "I guess I could take a break for a little while."

I give her my best smile. "I mean, everyone has to eat at some point, right? I promise, I won't keep you long. I don't want to be a distraction."

"You're not a distraction, Dax. I mean, I already burned myself today, so I probably should take a break." Chloe reaches toward the table behind her and grabs her keys and sunglasses before stepping into a pair of sandals. "Let's go."

She brushes past me in a whirl of citrus and blonde hair. That faint aroma pulls me right back to that night where I had my hands all over her. Where it was just the two of us in that room. No one else.

Fuck. I do not need to be sporting a boner at a picnic with my best friend.

"Where are we going?" Chloe asks as I hop into the truck after her.

"There's that cute park near downtown I thought we could go to. Do I need to swing by the store and buy you something for your burn?"

She holds up her bandaged finger. "I'm all taken care of."

"As long as you don't lose any fingers," I say.

"I won't." She slides her dark black sunglasses on and rests her feet on the dash as I steer us toward the city.

A silence settles over us. One that I'm not used to. Could things be weird because she wants to forget about what happened? How can you forget about your friend dry humping with you and getting off?

I don't know if that's possible.

I don't know what possessed me that night at the club, but it was like I was a different person. Drake went after what he wanted. And who he wanted.

Cora.

It's not a long trip to the park, but I don't want things to be awkward for even the short drive.

"How much did you get done today?" I ask. It's about the only thing I can come up with.

Chloe tucks a lock of hair behind her ear, resting her head against the back of the seat and turning to face me. "Not as much as I would have liked. I tried my first bracelet last night. I'm still learning the best way to get the charms onto each link in the most efficient way."

"Learning curve. You'll get there."

"I hope so. What if I have this dream that I want to open my own store but I'm actually terrible at it?"

"What makes you think that?" I ask, merging onto the highway.

"I've never run my own business before. What if I don't have a knack for it?"

"Then you'll take a class."

"Just like that?"

"What can I say? I won't let you give up."

Chloe reaches across the center console and squeezes my forearm. I ignore the zap of electricity that floods my veins.

"Thanks for believing in me."

"I'll be your first customer," I say, finding the exit we need.

As we pull up to the stoplight, Chloe turns to face me. "You already have a necklace. Maybe I can make you something else. Like a clover."

I beam back at her. "My very own good luck charm."

"Would you want gold or silver?"

"Silver."

"You got it. I'll do anything for you, Dax."

Like say yes to being my date to the team gala?

Jesus. I really need to get my shit together or I'm just going to blurt it out that I've been in love with her since high school. And the last thing I want to do is scare her off right now.

The park comes into view. Thank God.

"What a gorgeous day." Chloe hops out as soon as I park and turns her face to the sun. "Thanks for bringing me here. I probably would have stayed inside all day otherwise."

"What are friends for?" I smile, the picnic basket in one hand with the blanket thrown over my shoulder. "C'mon. Let's find a spot."

Even though it's in the middle of the day, it's busy. Sprawling green fields. Trees rustling in the slight wind. Bees buzzing around flower beds as we stroll down the sidewalk.

"How about right here?" Chloe asks.

"Looks good."

It's a quiet area with only a few other people spread out with books in hand. The perfect spot for the conversation I want to have.

"What'd you make for us?" she asks, throwing the blanket into the air with both hands and letting it fall into a perfectly neat square on the ground.

"Sandwiches."

She beams back at me. "Ham?"

I set the basket down, drop onto the blanket, and start to pull things out. I hand her the sandwich wrapped in brown butcher paper. "Of course."

"Did you—"

"Leave the mustard off? Of course. Bottle is in here. I know you don't like them to get soggy," I finish for her.

"It's like you know me or something."

I don't miss the blush that creeps up her cheeks as she kicks off her sandals and plops onto the covered ground.

I pull out a small bowl of fruit, some pita chips and hummus, and hand over the yellow bottle to her. She wastes no time pulling off a slice of the sourdough bread and covering one side in mustard.

"Did you save any for me?"

"There's plenty left." Chloe takes a hearty bite and smiles at me as she chews.

I grab the bottle and put some on my own sandwich. "Sure there is."

She leans over and pecks me on the cheek. "Thank you, Dax."

My entire body seizes up. One peck and I'm a goner. I don't know how I've made it this far in life keeping my emotions in check around her.

I give her a smile. What that smile tells her, I don't know, because she sets her meal down and brushes off her hands.

"Are you okay?"

"Why wouldn't I be okay?" I fire back.

"Because you look nervous. And you're never nervous."

Sunglasses hide my eyes from view. Of course she would still be able to tell I'm nervous. I mean, why wouldn't I be? Asking my best friend to take a chance on me when she ran out on my brother?

Why would I have anything to be nervous about?

Her eyes trail over every inch of me. From my black T-shirt to my tan shorts all the way to my scuffed-up Converse sneakers.

"Why do you think I'm nervous?"

She points to my hand resting on my knee. "Your fingers keep tapping."

"Am I that easy to read?" I shove a nervous hand through my hair.

"Yes."

Do I rip the Band-Aid off and just blurt it out, or do I ease her into this?

"Spill it, Dax."

Band-Aid it is.

"About the other night."

A flush creeps up her cheeks. "What about the other night?"

"Look, I know we said nothing would change, but it feels like it did."

"Yeah." This time, it's Chloe who looks nervous. Shit. Is she about to let me down gently? I don't know if I could bear it.

"I know we said it wouldn't," I rush out, "but it did. And I can't stop thinking about it. Or you. And I was wondering if you'd maybe, kind of, sort of, be interested in doing more of that."

She smiles at me. "As Drake and Cora or as Dax and Chloe?"

"You and me."

Chloe studies me before crawling over to sit on my lap. She kicks her legs out, and I rest my hand on her warm, soft skin.

"What would you and I look like?" She drags a finger along my jaw.

"Kind of like what we have now. Maybe a bit more of what we did at the club."

"Maybe with some kissing?"

She waggles her eyebrows at me.

"You want me to kiss you?"

"Yes, Dax. All I've been thinking about is how much I want you—"

I kiss her. I crush my mouth to hers and holy fuck. We're kissing.

And it's the best fucking thing of my life.

The taste of her. The feel of her. The sounds she's making.

I love every bit of it. When she gasps, I slip my tongue in her mouth. Her fingers dig into my biceps as we savor one another. We're in no hurry.

I have dreamed of this for God knows how long. It's better than I ever imagined.

"Wow." Chloe pulls pack, resting her forehead against mine.

"Yeah."

"What was the question you asked me?"

"About wanting to make this official." I smile at her. "And possibly coming with me to the team gala that's coming up in a few weeks."

"I think you have my answer."

"To which one?"

"To both."

"I think I missed it." I tap my lips. "Mind telling me again?"

She does just that. Telling me all afternoon how much she wants this.

Who knew having an adult conversation could be so easy?

Chapter Eighteen

CHLOE

"You know, when you suggested a date, this isn't quite what I had in mind."

"Want something fancier?" Dax asks.

"No. This is perfect." The sun is starting to dip closer to the river. People are milling around and heading across the bridge to Broadway. "Absolutely perfect first date."

I stab my fork into the box of to-go noodles we picked up after the game—a shutout for the Knights at 5-0, with Dax scoring two goals.

"Would we consider this our first date?" Dax asks.

"What else would it be?"

"The sex club."

"Dax." I bump his hip with mine. "We cannot tell people our first date was at a sex club!"

"Probably the most unique first date, don't you think?" He waggles his brows at me.

"I'm making it official. This is our first *first* date and nothing else. Just you and me and no one else."

"Okay." He drapes his arm around my shoulders, pulling me close. "And I'm glad it's officially this as our first date because I don't want to be around other people tonight."

The regular season started two weeks ago, and since that day in the park, Dax and I haven't had as much time together as we would have liked. Grabbing dinner from a food truck and walking along the river after his game? I'll take whatever I can get. And this is pretty perfect to me.

"Hey, great game, Dax!" someone calls out as we stroll along the river.

He waves in return. "Thanks, man."

"You know, you did have a really good game tonight." I wrap my arm around him as we keep walking.

"I could have done more."

"Stop it. You're allowed to give yourself more credit than that, at least with me. I know how hard you've been working and it's showing. Two goals and an assist in the third period? That's incredible."

Pink creeps up his cheeks. Even if I tell him to take the credit, it'll still be hard for him. "That was great teamwork."

"They're lucky to have you." I spot an empty bench ahead. "Want to sit?"

"Sure."

He drops a kiss on my cheek before I bound over to take a seat. Dax pulls me in close to him, every inch of his side touching mine. He wolfed down his own dinner before we even made it to the river—no doubt because of the game—and I relish being wrapped up in his arms like this.

It's the most innocent of touches, but it makes me feel alive. I can't remember the last time I felt something so good. So right.

Being with Dax just makes sense.

He heaves out a sigh, fingers trailing a warm path up

and down my arm. Goose bumps break out in his wake. I really could get used to his touch.

"About the gala tomorrow night…" Dax asks, breaking me from my thoughts.

"You're not uninviting me, are you?" I ask, wiping my hands and resting the empty container next to me.

"No, but I did hear that Genevieve might perform."

My eyes go wide. "Wait, really? I love her new song."

"Which one is that?" Dax asks. "You know I don't listen to her."

"It's 'Wildflower in the Weeds.' You know, *I'm a wildflower, blowing with the wind, never knowing where I'll be, take me as I am, a wildflower in the weeds?* That one." I sing the first few lines for him.

A knowing smile slides into place. "I know the song. I just wanted to see if you'd sing it for me."

I grab his shirt and pull him close. "It's a good thing you're cute."

"Only cute?"

"Cute. Hot. Sexy."

"Better."

He gives me a featherlight kiss that makes my insides sing with joy. My toes curl. If this is a hint of what's to come, I can't wait.

"Back to the gala. What'd you want to tell me?"

"Marcus said Harper and Stevie are going to get ready at the hotel if you want to join them. I figured I could get us a room there together to spend the night."

A sly smile slips onto my face. "Why does it feel like you're asking me to prom and then we're going to have sex?"

Dax bursts out laughing. "Only you, Chloe."

"What?" I lean back. "That's what it feels like. I never got the real prom experience. No corsage. Just a drunk guy who picked me up in a limo and then couldn't dance with me."

I don't need to tell Dax who it was. He already knows.

"Well then. I will try to right these wrongs that were done to you back in high school. Give you the true prom experience."

"Being with you is enough," I say. "Getting to dress up and be on your arm and maybe listen to my favorite singer? It'll be the perfect night."

Dax's warm hand cups my cheek. His brown eyes are soft as a small smile curls his mouth.

How could I have been so oblivious to how this man looks at me? Maybe I didn't want to believe it, but now that we're here, I don't know how I missed it.

The tender way Dax always looks at me makes me feel seen. This is what I've been missing for so many years. To sit with someone and know I'm cared for.

I never had that with Duncan. With Dax I've felt it every day we've been together, even the days we're apart.

I close the distance between the two of us, sealing my mouth over his. It's the sweetest kiss. One full of promise but also need. A hunger for this man that starts low in my belly and keeps growing as Dax deepens the kiss.

Each swipe of his tongue strikes the match that burns the fire inside of me. I lean into his touch. Craving more. My fingers play with the soft hairs at the nape of his neck. His thumb presses into the throbbing pulse of my neck.

"Dax." I pull away, breathless. "We can't do this here."

Lust fills his eyes. "You're saying I can't kiss you, Sunshine?"

"You better kiss me, Dax. All I want is for you to kiss me. But if we keep going…"

"Right. We can save it for tomorrow."

"It might be my favorite part."

Dax narrows his eyes at me. "Might be? What else could be your favorite?"

"Do I have to tell you?" I snicker.

"By not telling me, you did," he groans.

"Maybe if you can introduce me to Genevieve if she does perform, you'll be my favorite part."

"I'll see what I can do."

Chapter Nineteen

DAX

CHLOE
I'll see you later

DAX
Have fun getting ready with the girls

And you have fun bowling

Seriously, it must be so nice being a guy

Shower and get dressed

Way too easy

I'm sorry?

Yeah, yeah

You'd look beautiful even if you did nothing

I'll see you soon

Get a strike

And if I do?

You might get lucky later 😏

Damn. Now I really need to score

Smiling, I pocket my phone and hop out of my truck at the dingy bowling alley. Not sure why Marcus picked this place, but who am I to judge?

Pulling open the door, the stale scents of smoke and old beer greet me. Low lights flicker in the lobby as crashing pins explode.

"Hey, man."

A kid who can't be more than seventeen nods at me.

"I believe the reservation is under Evans. I'll need a pair of shoes."

"You got it."

I pass over my credit card, tell him my size, and grab the shoes from him as he points to the lanes behind him.

At the end of the alley, Marcus, Bode, and Jasper are already here. It shouldn't surprise me that Noah and Graham are running late. With an early practice this morning and nothing to do this afternoon, we thought it'd be a fun way to spend a few hours before the gala tonight.

"Thanks."

I wave at the kid who buries his face into his phone, ignoring me.

For a weekend afternoon, it's not crowded. A few families are in the arcade, and what appears to be a bowling team is practicing in a few of the center lanes.

"About time you got here," Jasper barks at me. "I'm ready to get this over with."

"What's got you all knotted up?" Bode asks, lightly punching him in the shoulder.

"Nothing. Just…who decided on bowling?" Jasper grumbles.

"You know, you really need to get laid," Noah says, coming up behind him. "It would help with all that tension you're carrying around."

"Fuck off," he fires back. "I'm doing just fine."

"Are you worried you're going to lose?" Noah pokes. "I mean, I am an excellent bowler."

"Want to bet on it?" Jasper asks.

"You know, this isn't what I had in mind when I suggested we all go out together before the gala," Marcus says.

"We're all competitive. What did you expect?" I laugh.

"If you didn't want them betting, you should have picked a bar," Graham says.

"Nah. We're past those days," Bode says.

Everyone stops, staring at him.

"I never thought I'd hear you utter those words," Jasper tells him.

"Fuck off."

"Seriously," Jasper continues, "who would have seen the day that Bode is all loved up before Dax and me here."

Bode flips him off. "Well, when you find someone like Stevie, it's hard not to be."

"Technically, Chloe and I are seeing each other," I say.

"Technically?" Marcus questions. "I don't think there's any technically about it."

Noah drapes an arm around my shoulders. "I'm glad Chloe found you after that douchebag."

"Are you able to call his brother a douchebag?" Graham asks. "At least to his face?"

"Yes." Noah and I answer at the same time.

"I don't think she really 'found' him," Marcus states. "Dax has always been around. I guess she finally noticed him."

"Gee, thanks." I roll my eyes at him.

"What? It's true." Marcus shrugs. "It's not a bad thing. You two are perfect together and I'm happy for you."

"Which, speaking of that douche nozzle," Noah says, "did you see Detroit picked him up?"

"Oh, I saw," I confirm. "I hope they know what they're getting into."

"You know we'll be playing them in a couple of weeks," Jasper says.

"I know."

"Think you'll be able to keep it together and not punch him in the face after what he did to Chloe?" Noah asks. "I'd like to punch him for what he did to my sister."

"Maybe if he hadn't, she wouldn't be with Cash," Graham says.

Noah winces. "I really don't want to talk about my sister and her love life."

"Why don't we start bowling?" I ask. I do not want my love life—or anyone else's—to be the focus of conversation today. For a group of guys, there is far too much attention on our love lives. I don't know how it happened, but all of us have gone from going out to the bars to bowling because it's the tamer of activities we can do together.

"How are we doing this?" Noah asks. "Three versus three?"

"Yes," Marcus says. "And you and Graham are on the same team."

"Hey!" They both look affronted.

"Why can't we be on separate teams? We're always together," Graham says.

"Do you have a problem always being together?" Noah asks him.

"What if I wanted to kick your ass tonight?" He quirks a brow at him.

"What if I wanted your ass in other ways?" Noah fires back.

"Is this foreplay? Because if so, there are children around," Bode tells them. "Keep it in your pants."

"Do you think he's jealous that we're here together and Stevie isn't?" Noah ignores him.

"Oh, definitely," Graham says, slinging an arm around him. "He'll see her later."

"Would you two be nice to him? I don't want him to leave before we play." Marcus points a finger at each of them.

"Okay, fine."

I drop into a seat to untie my shoes and put on the hard bowling shoes. Marcus types our names into the screen as we get going.

"Are we betting on this?" I ask, as Noah takes the seat next to me. Bode, Graham, and Jasper are ready to go.

"I say whichever team wins gets to pick the next team outing," Bode says.

Marcus grins at him as he picks up his orange ball. "Which means this is going to become a regular thing. Glad I got you on board."

Bode rolls his eyes back at him. "Yeah, yeah. It's not like it's a hardship to spend time with you idiots."

"Aww, he really loves us." Jasper ruffles his hair as he grabs a ball and approaches the line. Without missing a beat, he lines up his shot and sends the ball spinning down the lane. The crack echoes loudly as all ten pins come crashing down.

"Damn. Why isn't he on our team?" I ask.

"Hey." Noah nudges me in the side. "We're good."

Marcus takes his turn, getting a gutter ball.

"We are?" I quirk a brow at him.

"Well, some of us."

"Sorry," Marcus says, walking back to wait for the return to spit his ball out. "I forgot I can actually try."

Bode groans from his spot. "Does this mean I'm going to have to lose on purpose when Caleb is old enough to bowl?"

"If you don't want him complaining about losing, then yes," Marcus tells him. This time, he manages to get five pins down.

A waiter comes around and takes our food and drink orders as the game continues. I get a measly three pins down on my first turn, while Noah puts up two goose eggs.

Meanwhile, the other team is crushing us. They're already up by twenty-five points.

"You know, I really can get on board with this whole bowling thing," Jasper says.

"Only because you're on the winning team," Noah goads. Jasper ignores him, pulling out his phone, an annoyed look washing over his face.

"What's wrong with you?" Noah asks.

"Nothing," Jasper bites back.

"You seem more annoyed than usual."

"Maybe because you're bugging me?" Jasper clarifies.

"He's right. You were happy and now you're grumpy," Bode says, ganging up on him.

"Maybe it's because I have to hang out with you assholes," Jasper throws back at Bode.

Our waiter sets down two pitchers of beer and six glasses. I pour a round of drinks, watching as the guys bicker back and forth.

"Do you think he met someone?" Marcus whispers out of the corner of his mouth.

"Probably has to do with why he always texts us random things," I answer.

"There's no way Jasper would start dating someone and not tell us, right?" Noah asks.

"I mean, he's always been the quiet type," I reply.

It wouldn't surprise me if Jasper were to start dating someone and not tell us. Marcus couldn't keep the dopey grin off his face when he and Harper got back together. Stevie and Caleb are all Bode talks about.

Me?

I've never been one to hide my feelings. But then again, I've never really had a serious girlfriend before. There have been a few, but no one that I felt the need to tell the guys about.

Except Chloe.

Chloe is the exception to every rule.

The guys didn't bat an eye when I told them about me and Chloe. Our feelings are the real deal.

Marcus sets his drink down, swiping a nacho and heading back to the ball return. "Okay, leave Jasper alone. If he wants to ignore us and not tell us what is going on with his personal life, we won't hold it against him. Now, I'm ready to beat you assholes."

Instead, Marcus gets two gutter balls in a row.

"You're going to beat us, huh?" Graham prods.

Noah flips him off as he splits the pins.

"Okay, we are definitely not bowling next time," I tell them as I follow Marcus's lead and throw two gutter balls.

"Oh, we are totally doing this again," Bode says. "Maybe we should make it a date night."

"Really?" I quirk a brow at him. "It's still weird to hear you say things like that."

"Stevie would love it." Bode pulls out his phone, smiling. "Besides, it looks like the girls like each other."

My own phone buzzes and I pull it out. There's a group text with me, the three women, Marcus, and Bode. The three of them are holding champagne, smiling at the camera.

"Yeah, it looks like they're getting along great," I say.

"As long as we do it in the next few weeks. Childcare is going to get hard because the grandmas have a cruise in November."

"Ahh, the life of a parent." Marcus laughs. "I can't wait until the girls are old enough to babysit."

"They'd be good influences on Caleb. Make sure he eats his vegetables," I tell them.

"Hey. Caleb is the most perfect kid there is." Bode whacks me on the chest. "Watch it."

"Sorry." I throw my hands up, heading to take my turn.

The ball leaves my hand on a perfect spin, crashing into the pins and knocking all ten down.

"Hell yeah!" I pump my arms in victory. "See if you guys win now."

Jasper does a slow clap. "Great job. You're still down by forty."

"Yeah, yeah." I roll my eyes at him as I grab my beer and toast with Marcus. "I'll take one perfect frame."

Even if we're losing and they pick the next activity, I wouldn't mind this being a date night with the guys and our partners.

I love that we're all here together while the girls are getting ready for the big gala tonight.

I never thought that this was going to be what a day could look like. Hanging with the guys and then going out with all of us together, Chloe included.

If it's up to me, Chloe will be around for a long time. Forever, I hope.

Chapter Twenty

CHLOE

DAX

I can't wait to see you tonight

CHLOE

I saw you this morning

I know

But I miss you already

Is that cheesy?

No

Because I miss you too

I can't wait to see you in your dress

Ditto

You can't wait to see you in your dress too?

I meant I can't wait to see you in your tux

I already want to peel you out of it

Patience, Dax. Patience

<<tick tock gif>>

S tuffing my phone in my purse, I grab the bags from the front seat of my car and hand the keys over to the valet.

"Welcome to the Nashville Grande. We hope you enjoy your stay."

"Thank you."

I smile at the young kid as he gets into the driver seat and drives off in my old car. The hotel where the event is being held tonight lives up to its name.

Everything about this hotel is grand, from the gilded fountain to the marble lobby. Everything is ornate right down to the flickering sconces lining the columns of the two-story entryway.

Swinging by the front desk, I get the room key that's waiting for me and take the elevator to Harper's room.

When Dax told me the girls invited me to get ready with them for tonight's big event, I was excited. It's been awhile since I've had any girlfriends other that Erica. With Duncan, it was all about him. I became so swept up in him, that it seems I lost almost all my friends. They moved on with their lives without me.

I can't blame them. But I don't want to squander the opportunity to meet new people. Especially people so important to Dax's friends.

When the elevator opens onto the seventh floor, I

follow the sign to her room. I know Dax got a room for tonight, so we won't have to drive home.

I can't wait to *finally* spend the night with him.

Knocking on the door, it swings open to reveal a smiling blonde woman with her hair in rollers. I've never met her before. Having been with Duncan, I never really spent any time with Dax and his teammates. Especially their significant others.

"Hi. You must be Chloe."

"That's me. And are you Harper or Stevie?"

"Harper. Stevie's in the bathroom doing her makeup." She beckons me in and shuts the door behind me.

A brunette walks out into the hallway in a robe.

"Chloe. Hi."

"Hi. That must mean you're Stevie."

"That's me. I'm so glad you could come hang out with us today."

"Me too."

I drop my bags onto a seat and look around the room. When Dax told me the guys go all out for this, he wasn't kidding. A couch sits on one side of the living room with a small kitchenette making up the other side. Music plays through the TV—one of Genevieve's hits—and large floor-to-ceiling windows look out over the Nashville skyline. A door tucked in the back of the room leads to what I'm guessing is the bedroom.

"I really appreciate you two inviting me over to get ready with you."

Harper walks into the kitchen and grabs a bucket with a chilling bottle of champagne. "It's nice that Dax finally has someone to bring around. I worry about him."

"You do?" I ask, taking the proffered glass of bubbly.

"All the guys do. They were worried he'd never find someone because he was hung up on you," Harper says.

"Hung up on me?"

"Crap. Did you not know?" Harper casts a worried look Stevie's way. "I mean, that's what Marcus said and he was a mess at your…well, your non-wedding day now."

"I guess I was always too wrapped up in Duncan to see what was right in front of my face."

"We've all been taken by someone that's not good for us. I know I have," Stevie says. "And you two are together now. That's all that matters."

"Don't I know it." I shake my head, sipping on my drink. "And you're not the first person to point out Dax's feelings toward me."

"I think you got the better end of that deal," Harper says. "Marcus told me what happened and I still can't believe it. I'm sorry you had to go through all of that."

I wave them off. "It's in the past now. I don't want to talk about *him* tonight. Tonight is all about the gala and our men."

"I'll drink to that." Stevie raises her glass. "To new and old friends."

"Cheers," we echo, snapping a quick selfie to send to the guys.

I start to unpack my things to get ready as Harper and Stevie tell me about their families.

"Want help with your hair?" Harper asks. "I'm so used to curling the girls' hair now, I'm a natural."

"If you're sure."

"Absolutely. Sit down and tell me how you met Dax," Harper says, patting the stool we moved into the bathroom.

"We met in high school. The two of us were in the same homeroom our freshmen year and we've been friends ever since. Dax has been in my life almost as long as he wasn't."

"That's sweet," Harper says, fishing out a lock of hair and twisting it around the hot iron. "Most of my friends I met in college or while teaching."

"It's so hard to make friends as an adult," Stevie says. "I don't know how we're expected to meet people when all we do is work."

"You've got that right," I say. "And now that I'm starting my own business, there are some days I never leave the house."

"Bode said you're making jewelry?" Stevie asks, touching up her eyeliner.

"I am. I've always wanted to do it, and after everything that happened, I figured why not?"

"Can you show us what you've made?" Harper asks, finishing one side of my hair and moving on to the back.

Grabbing my phone from my leggings pocket, I tap into the album of my most recent creations. "A lot of them are still in progress and need a final polish, but I love designing rings the most. I've just started working on bracelets and charms."

"You made those?" Stevie peers over Harper's shoulder as they flip through the photos. "These are amazing, Chloe."

"Are you taking orders? Because I would love to get some of these for myself and the girls," Harper says. "You are talented."

"Thanks. Once I figure everything out order-wise, I will get you hooked up."

"You better," Harper reiterates. "I want to say I had a ring from Chloe before she hit it big."

I laugh. "I don't know if anyone will be saying that, but we'll see."

"Well, I'm getting in on this too. I only wish we had some to wear tonight," Stevie laments.

"Maybe for the next gala," Harper says. "Because I have a feeling you'll be coming to next year's."

"Is this an annual thing?" I ask.

"They want to make it that way," Stevie replies. "The owner's granddaughter had a pretty severe leg break from what Bode told me, and he was blown away by all they did for her, so he is making it his mission to support the hospital now."

"Is she okay?"

She nods. "She's doing great and apparently wants to try out for the hockey club in her school."

"I love that she wants to play hockey. Do your girls want to play?" I ask Harper.

"No. One loves chess and the other is currently into knitting with her Gigi. Now our son, Jamie, he might play hockey, but he's three, so we've got a few years."

"Not if Marcus has anything to say about it. Bode is already planning on getting Caleb into skates as soon as he can."

I love listening to the two of them talk about their partners and families. Every so often, they mention the guys, and it seems like they're their own little family unit.

"All set," Harper exclaims.

"I can't believe how fast you did that." I fluff my curls before setting them with hairspray.

"When you have twin girls that are always late, you learn how to move things along." She laughs.

"Oh!" Stevie gasps. "The guys will be here soon. We need to get dressed."

"We don't want to be late. We'll never hear the end of it," Harper says. "Chloe, there's another bedroom through that door if you want to change in there. I can change in the bathroom if you want the other room, Stevie."

"Got it."

Grabbing my dress bag, I head into the empty room to change.

I don't know why I ever kept this dress—a bridesmaid's dress for one of Duncan's college friends whose wedding I was in—but I could never seem to part with it.

I loved the way I felt in it.

Sexy. Beautiful. Like I could take on the world.

Shimmying into my undergarments, I pull the dress on and finagle the zipper closed.

I step into my strappy heels and add a spritz of perfume to my wrists and behind my ears. Fluffing my hair one last time, I head back out into the living room.

"Chloe, Dax is going to lose his mind when he sees you in this dress." Harper whistles as I step out of the bedroom. "I mean, wow."

"It's not too much?" I ask, rubbing my hands down the front of the satiny material. "It was from a wedding I was in a few years back and I never wanted to get rid of it just in case."

"It's a good thing you didn't. You look amazing," Stevie says.

"Thanks," I say, a blush creeping up my cheeks.

I check myself out in the full-length mirror. A thin row of sequins lines the sweetheart neckline. It's form-fitting all the way through, but has an almost scandalous thigh-high slit on one side. More sequins line the slit, catching the light to make the dress pop.

"Both of you look gorgeous too."

Stevie is in a short, black dress with a plunging neckline and Harper is in a form-fitting gold dress that dips low in the back.

"The boys won't know what hit them."

I smile at the two of them.

I can't wait for tonight and everything it holds. It's

already been the best start to this night, hanging out with these two women that I can now call friends, and getting to spend the rest of the evening with Dax.

I only wish we could fast forward to the end.

Because I can't wait to be with Dax in every way.

Chapter Twenty-One

DAX

"Is this stupid? It feels stupid."

I'm questioning myself yet again as the guys and I ride up the elevator car to the floor where the girls are getting ready.

"Relax. She is going to love it." Marcus claps me on the shoulder. "I only wish I'd thought of it."

I adjust my bowtie in the mirrored wall of the car.

I'm nervous. I know it's Chloe, but I never went to prom or took a girl to a dance. By the time I could go, I was traveling for hockey. That took priority for me.

"Seriously. You're making us look bad," Bode chimes in.

"Sorry."

The elevator dings and we get out, heading toward Harper's room. With each step, my nerves ratchet up higher and higher.

I can't wait to see what Chloe is wearing. I know she said she had something to wear that I would love, so I'm ready.

Marcus is knocking on the door, and based on his reaction when it opens, it's Harper.

"You look amazing."

I follow Marcus and Bode inside. The living room of the suite is scattered with clothes and makeup containers along with an empty bottle of champagne and the remnants of lunch.

Chloe, swiping on one last coat of lip gloss, stops me in my tracks.

She is a vision in a long, strapless black dress with a thigh-high slit. The fabric around the slit is dotted in black sequins, as is the material around her chest. It's subtle, but perfect. Her long blonde hair is flowing in bouncy curls.

"Wow. Just…wow."

She turns to face me, a bright smile on her face. "Hi."

"You look incredible, Sunshine." I drop a quick kiss on her lips, not wanting to ruin her makeup.

"Not so bad yourself." She smooths a hand down the front of my tux. "It's annoying you guys went bowling after practice this morning and it takes you all of ten minutes to shower and get ready."

"Sorry." I pull the plastic container from behind my back. "Would this help make up for it?"

"You really got me one?" Chloe's hands fly to her mouth in surprise.

"If I could have gotten away with a limo, I would have."

I crack open the plastic container and pull out the corsage, made up of three white roses and baby's breath. I slide the band around her wrist.

"Dax. This is perfect." She pulls me in for a kiss, not caring that we're not the only people in the room.

I couldn't care less either because all I want is this woman in my arms.

Until someone clears their throat.

"We have donors we need to go impress," Marcus says.

"Right."

I pull away from Chloe, wiping the smear of pink gloss from my lips. Crimson creeps up her cheeks.

"I guess we better get downstairs," Chloe whispers.

I lean close, my breath ghosting her ear. "Just wait until later tonight."

A shudder racks her body as I take her hand in mine and follow everyone else out of the room.

"Where are the other guys?" Stevie asks.

She's wrapped in Bode's arms as we wait for the elevator.

"They're downstairs," I say, keeping my eyes on the gorgeous woman next to me as we step into the elevator.

I don't know how I got so lucky to have this woman take a chance on me. If I hadn't been worried about her that night at the club and gone to check on her, would we be here right now?

Would I be able to pull her in my arms and press a kiss to her neck as we ride down?

All I know is I'm glad I had the balls to go that night because I would be missing out on this.

When we get to the lobby, the guys exit and we follow a few paces behind.

"You look gorgeous tonight," I tell her again. "I'm the luckiest guy in the world."

"I think I might have the most handsome guy with me tonight."

I steal one more kiss before we enter the ballroom.

"This looks incredible."

Tall vases of flowers encircled by small, flickering candles sit on each table. Long swaths of white fabric hang from the walls and ceiling with glittering lights behind them. People are milling about as servers in white jackets serve hors d'oeuvres and glasses of champagne.

"They really go all out, don't they?" Chloe asks, giving my hand a tighter squeeze.

"Helps to get bigger donations," I whisper, dropping her hand to take two glasses of champagne from a passing server.

"Just tell me what I need to do and I'll do it."

I quirk a brow at her. "Does that only apply in here?"

"Dax!" she hisses, taking a sip of her drink. "You can't say that."

"Why not?" I grin down at her, pulling her close.

"Because we have a long night ahead of us and I don't need to be thinking about *that* right now."

"Later." I kiss her cheek. "I can't wait for later."

Our group spreads out, making the rounds as we talk to the guests. Even though it's early in the season, we hear how great the team is looking. I introduce Chloe and proudly tell them about her new business. No reason I can't try and help her business while helping the Knights, right?

"You know, you don't have to keep selling these people on my business," Chloe tells me as we take our seats for dinner.

"Who says I can't?" I grin. "I think I've gotten you at least four different people who want to host a jewelry party at their house."

Chloe tries to fight the smile, but she can't. "It is exciting that they want me to come, right?"

"See?" I kiss her because I can. "Let me be your hype guy."

Chloe extends her arm behind my chair. "And I'll be your hype girl while you're on the ice. I'll be the best cheerleader out there."

"Hey now," Harper interrupts. "Don't let the girls hear you say that. They proudly wear that crown for their dad."

Chloe laughs. "They can be Marcus's biggest fan. I'm Dax's."

Bode nudges me in the side while Harper and Chloe discuss the next game they'll go to.

"It seems like she's really into you."

"Thanks, I think?"

Bode drops his voice lower. "I was worried because she was with Duncan and might just need to fill the void—"

"Again, thanks?" I ask.

"Hold on." He smacks me in the shoulder. "But she really likes you. I was looking out for you, but I think you're good."

I sneak a peek at Chloe. "Yeah, I'm good."

"Good."

"Good evening, everyone." The team owner calls everyone's attention to the stage, where a spotlight shines down on him. "I want to thank you all for joining us here tonight to raise money for the local children's hospital. I know how much it means to them that we host this event, so I urge you to open up those pocketbooks during the silent auction to help us this evening. I don't want to monopolize your time, so enjoy your dinner and I'll be back with a surprise before the dancing starts."

Everyone claps as Chloe leans over. "Okay, that has to be Genevieve."

"I don't want to get my hopes up." Stevie leans across Bode to talk to Chloe. "Do you really think it's going to be her?"

Chloe nods as a plate is set in front of her. "I mean, it has to be, right? Wouldn't they just say otherwise?"

"I really hope so," Harper says from Chloe's other side. "I've never gotten to see her perform live."

"Me either," Chloe says. "This would make the best night if she did."

"*That* would make it the best night?" I whisper, grabbing a knife and cutting into my chicken.

She rests her chin on my shoulder, staring up at me. "Well, it'd make the night better. It's already pretty great."

"Yeah."

We all eat our chicken—rather dry, if I do say so myself—chatting about our upcoming game and road trip while the girls talk about what else the surprise could be.

I love that they bonded so quickly. I've only met Harper and Stevie a few times, but I knew that they'd get along.

After dinner is cleared out, the tables are moved away to make room for the dance floor, while a dessert bar is spread along another table against the wall.

Before anyone can go far, Coach Andrews takes the stage.

"Hi everyone. I'll keep this short and sweet because I get to introduce the big surprise tonight. I think everyone knows her, but please welcome to the stage Genevieve!"

"It's her!" Chloe smacks me on the arm as we head toward the dance floor. "Oh my God!"

"This is so cool!" Harper grabs Chloe's arm and drags her and Bode closer to the stage.

"Should we go up there with them?" I ask Marcus as Jasper joins us.

"Nah. Let them enjoy it. I'm fine standing back here."

Dropping an elbow onto the cocktail table, I listen as the music starts. It's a song I don't recognize, but I recognize her.

Genevieve is the biggest pop star in the world right now. How they got her to come perform here, I don't know. Jasper's jaw drops as he takes in the curvy star. His eyes are focused only on her.

In a black, one-shoulder dress with a cut-out on the side, glittery fabric flows down from her shoulder. Long, silver earrings catch the light as she moves around the stage.

She's powerful and captivating while she's performing. But my eyes aren't looking at her. They're looking for the woman dancing to the music up front with a smile lighting up her face.

I don't know the lyrics to this song, but she's talking about finding the right person to fall in love with at the wrong time.

Huh. I guess you could say that was what happened with me and Chloe. All these years in each other's lives, but nothing happening until she left my brother.

I sip my drink, not bothering to hide my happiness. Because if it weren't for him being a dick, I wouldn't be here with her right now.

The song ends, and she starts singing another one that I recognize. Given the fact that Chloe loves her, I know most of these songs.

When there's a break in the set, the girls come back up to the table, smiles on their flushed faces.

"Having fun out there?" I ask, wrapping an arm around Chloe.

"It's so cool getting to see her perform like this," she says.

"She's amazing," Harper agrees. "We're going to have to get tickets to her next show. Whenever that might be."

"Count me in," Stevie says. "I'd love to go."

Before Chloe can say anything, her jaw drops. Following her gaze, I know why. The pop star in question is walking our way.

"Hi there." Genevieve comes up to our table. "I'm Genevieve. It's nice to meet you all."

Jasper snorts next to me and Bode elbows him in the side. "What? It's not like she needs to introduce herself when she's the world's biggest pop star."

She smiles back at him. "It's only polite."

"More polite than him." Bode laughs.

"It's nice to meet you…" Genevieve holds her hand out toward him.

"Jasper. But we've met before. When you sang the national anthem at our game."

She flashes an award-winning smile at him. "I think I'd remember if I'd met one of the Knights' greatest players."

"Then you clearly haven't met Jasper," Bode jokes.

"Ouch. You going to let him talk to you like that?" Genevieve fires toward Jasper. "I think you should respect your elders."

"He's not that much older," Bode says.

"We're meeting the world's biggest pop star and you guys are arguing over who is older?" Harper shakes her head. "I'm sorry, we can't take these guys anywhere."

"They're always like this," Stevie confirms. "But we love them anyway."

"They sound like keepers," Genevieve says.

"That they are," Chloe says, smiling over at me.

"Well, it was nice to meet you all. I was taking a quick break but need to get back up on stage." She throws up a peace sign. "Got to go."

"Who says that?" Noah laughs as she retreats.

"Holy shit," Jasper says, eyes flying to the space vacated by the pop star.

"What?" I ask.

"It's her."

"Her who?" Marcus asks.

"*Her*," he reiterates.

"Okay, you saying 'her' again doesn't help me know who her is," Marcus says.

"I have to go."

Jasper runs from the room before we can get any more information from him.

"Okay, that was weird, right?" Noah asks, throwing his thumb in the direction of where Jasper ran off.

"Even for Jasper, that was weird," Bode says. "Is he dating someone that we don't know about?"

"It sounds like it," Stevie says. "But he looked surprised by whoever this her is."

"Think we should go after him and see if he's okay?" Graham asks.

"Let him be for now." Harper pats him on the arm. "If he's not telling you guys he's seeing someone, there must be a reason."

"Hey!" we all answer, affronted, at the same time.

"Why wouldn't he tell us?" Marcus asks.

"Yeah, I'm offended that he thinks he can't tell us," Bode says.

"It's not like we'd give him shit about it," I say.

Harper and Stevie exchange a look and laugh. "I can't believe you all think that. You're the biggest bunch of gossips. You love each other, but you would give him so much grief over a new girl."

"We would not," Noah states.

"I mean, we definitely would," Graham argues.

"Whose side are you on?" Noah elbows him in the side.

"I'm just saying. I know us, and Jasper would take a lot of heat for this one," Graham says.

"I'm with Harper and Stevie," Chloe says. "My guess is it's new and he doesn't want you guys getting in his head."

"We would be nothing but supportive," Marcus says. "We always are."

"I mean, after we gave him shit for not telling us," Bode says. "After all the crap he's given us over the years? He'd deserve it."

"Want to dance?" I ask Chloe.

If Jasper wants to keep quiet on his love life, I'll let him have it. Right now, all I care about is Chloe.

"Yes."

Linking hands with her, I lead her onto the dance floor. I don't know this song, but I don't care. Holding the woman I love more than anything close, we sway to the music.

"Thanks for coming with me tonight." I twirl a lock of soft hair around my finger.

"It's been fun, but…"

"But what?" I step back, looking down into her eyes.

Bright blue eyes filled with need.

"I'm ready to get out of here."

At this moment, it's only the two of us in this ballroom. And I want to be anywhere but here.

"Let's go."

Chapter Twenty-Two

CHLOE

Tension brims and swirls on the longest elevator ride known to humankind. Dax stands on one side of the small car, hands in his pockets, while I wait on the other.

I don't think I've ever seen Dax look as sexy as when he's wearing a tux. And all I want to do is rip it off of him.

"Is your tux rented?"

"Why are you asking?" He looks confused.

Pushing off the gold hand railing, I close the distance between us. I finger the studs on his starched shirt. "Because you look so good in this that I'm ready to tear it off you."

He tugs me in close, hands skimming the top of my ass. "We could get in trouble if we did that in here."

"Too bad we can't go somewhere else where it would be okay." I quirk a brow at him.

"That would take way too long to get there. And I've been patient all night."

"You have, have you?"

I drag a finger along his smooth jaw. A shudder racks my body at the thought of feeling his face between my legs.

"It was a trial in patience, Chloe." Dax presses his lips just below my ear. "Seeing you in this dress? All I've wanted to do is peel you out of it. See what's hiding underneath."

"Dax," I moan, digging my fingers into his pecs. "I need you."

He trails his lips up and down my neck. Hot, wet kisses that ignite the fire in my core. "Almost there, Sunshine. Just a few—"

The elevator dings and I hurry out, not wanting to wait a second longer.

Dax, it seems, is in no hurry as he strolls behind me.

"Would you hurry up?" I snap my fingers at him.

"You have someplace you need to be?" He stops, fidgeting with his shirt cuffs.

"If you don't hurry up, Dax Fletcher, I am going to go into that room and start myself."

That gets his attention. "Is that supposed to be a punishment, Chloe? Because it doesn't sound like it."

"You are—"

What I was going to say is quickly forgotten as Dax hurries toward me and kisses me like I've never been kissed before.

He swallows my gasp, tangling his tongue with mine as he backs us toward our destination. We both fight for control as I cling to him for dear life.

Every nerve ending in my body is on fire and ready to explode at his taste. My back hits a wall, but we don't stop. If anything, it urges Dax on.

He thrusts a leg between mine, and I grind down on him as his lips move along my jaw. Featherlight kisses make me want to explode.

"Dax, I—"

"Yeah?" He tugs my earlobe between his teeth. "What do you want?"

"To be naked under you and feel you inside me."

"You don't like this?" He drags a finger along my exposed thigh.

"We've already done this. I want—"

"Tell me what you want."

It's a demand.

"I want your mouth on me as I come on your tongue."

"What else?" He flicks his tongue against the soft flesh of my ear and it makes me dizzy with lust.

"To feel your dick stretch me while you fuck me."

Dax pulls back, grabbing my hand and pulling me after him. "You should know something by now, Sunshine."

"What's that?"

"I'll always give you whatever you want."

Waving the key over the card reader, it flashes green and Dax pulls me in after him. The room is dark, except for the lights from the street flooding in from down below.

"Tell me more, Chloe." His voice is gravelly, deep. I've never heard it that way before. It goes right to my pussy, amping up my desire for this man.

"More of what?"

"What exactly do you want me to do to you right now?"

I spin, collecting my hair over one shoulder. "I want you to undress me."

The air is thick as Dax closes the distance between us and presses into me from behind. I gasp at the feel of his hard cock digging into my ass.

I don't think the humping at the club gave me a good idea of his size. But now? Dax is going to split me wide open and I can't wait.

He takes his time, dragging his fingers along my neck and shoulder. Tracing circles on my exposed back.

The snick of the zipper echoes in the room as he drags it down, millimeter by slow millimeter. His lips follow the path, getting lower and lower.

"Step out."

I kick the material to the side as he pulls me back against him. Strong hands roam up and down my sides.

"Do you know how long I've wanted to feel you like this, Chloe?"

"How long?" I whisper, peering up at him over my shoulder.

His eyes are tender, yet filled with lust and desire at the same time. "Longer than you can imagine."

Sweeping me into his arms, Dax drops me in the center of the bed before crawling over my body and straddling my hips.

"What are you going to do next?" I ask.

In nothing but my bra, underwear, and heels, it should feel weird to be like this with Dax—but it doesn't.

My only regret right now is that we haven't been doing this longer. Because as his deft fingers work the studs of his shirt, exposing his abs, I want to lick each and every one of them.

"Seems like you might want to do something." His lips quirk up into a sly smile.

Flipping our positions, I straddle Dax. His face is full of shock as I run my hands over his hard muscles.

Covering his body with mine, I drag my breasts over his chest as I whisper, "This."

Taking my time to savor his body, I kiss, nip, and suck my way down his neck. Over his hard pecs. Down the lines carved into his abs. The V's sneaking out from his pants.

I have never let myself ogle Dax, but tonight I am. I

am taking in every bit of this man that looks like he was chiseled from the finest marble.

"Chloe. Fuck."

"Not yet. I'm not done yet."

Dax's skin is warm and taut. He's writhing under my touch.

"I don't know how much longer I can wait," he bites out.

Kneeling between his spread legs, I run a finger along his hard cock. "You want me now?"

"I've always wanted you," he confesses. "But right now, I want you riding me."

I don't take my eyes off him as I grab his belt and undo the clasp. Unfasten the button and slide the zipper down.

"Up."

He lifts his hips so I can pull his pants down, taking his shoes and socks with them. In nothing but his undone shirt and black boxer briefs, I have to bite down on my lip to keep from jumping him. Strong thighs have a light dusting of hair as I crawl my way back up his body to relieve him of his briefs.

And when I do?

"Holy shit. You're huge."

Dax, my quiet, soft-spoken best friend, has the biggest dick I think I've ever seen in my life.

"It'll fit." He smirks.

"Are you sure?"

Beckoning me up with a finger, Dax pulls my body over his and kisses me. Hands sliding under the material of my underwear, he moves me over his cock. I moan and purr as the two of us make out like we have all the time in the world.

Dax flips us and hovers over me, eyes darker than I've ever seen them.

"What are you going to do now?" I stare down at his kiss-swollen lips.

Moving down my body, he pulls my underwear off and tosses them behind him. "I'm going to get a taste of you. Make you come on my tongue before you come on my dick."

My eyes don't leave his as he positions himself between my legs. He breathes me in, nose dragging through my wet folds.

"Dax," I whine.

"Patience, Sunshine. I want to remember everything about this moment."

"Like?"

"Like how good you smell. How soft your skin is. The way you look laid out for me. Fuck, I want to etch every single part of your body into my memory so I never forget."

"Can you do it after you make me come?" I plead, throwing my arm over my eyes.

I'm wet, greedy, and need this man to make me come like I've never come before in my life.

"Okay."

"Okay?" I peer up at him. "Just like that?"

"Just like that," he agrees. "Because I'll give you whatever you want."

This time, he swipes his tongue through my dripping pussy.

"Oh my God!" I arch off the bed at the first swipe.

His fingers dig into my thighs as he holds me open to him. He wastes no time devouring me like I'm his last meal on earth.

I push my fingers into his hair, holding on for dear life. His finger strums my clit as he lifts my hips higher off the bed.

"Oh my God. Oh my God."

I repeat it over and over again as Dax works me over like a fine-tuned instrument. It's like he knows exactly what to do to make me explode for him.

"I'm so close, Dax. So close."

He pushes two fingers inside of me and sucks onto my clit. I bite into my lip to keep from crying out because I want to draw out my pleasure a little longer. Feel his mouth on me.

"That's it, Sunshine. Yes. Come for me."

This time, he pushes three fingers inside of me as he rolls his tongue in a complicated maneuver over my clit.

It's all I need to be pulled under the weight of my release.

"Dax!" My thighs squeeze his head as my orgasm takes over. It feels endless. Wave after tidal wave of pleasure pulls me under. There's no better feeling as I relish the bliss coursing through me.

One high heel dangles from my foot and the other is off completely. My body is limp from how hard I came.

"Think you have one more in you?" He gives himself a long, slow stroke.

I cover his hand with mine. "For you? Yes."

I want nothing more than to feel that cock of his inside me and let him make me come again. Fill me so full that I know nothing but Dax and Dax alone.

Dax fishes his wallet out and plucks a condom from it before rolling it down his hard length. Down every single last inch that I still don't think will fit inside me.

"It'll fit, I promise."

My eyes snap to his. An easy smile plays on his gorgeous lips.

"How is it that you know what I'm thinking?"

"I know you, Chloe. You're easy to read."

"Then what am I thinking right now?"

"How annoyingly charming I am and how that bothers you because you want me inside of you."

"Damn. You are good."

Dax lowers himself over me, taking my lips in a sweet kiss as he rolls his hips through my pussy. My nails dig into his back, urging him on.

"Ready?" he whispers, kissing the corner of my mouth.

"Yes."

Lining himself up, he pushes inside, stopping every few inches to let me adjust.

And wow. Do I ever need to adjust.

"That's it, Sunshine. You're doing good." He reaches between us, fingering my clit. It sends my world tilting off axis even more.

His words of praise and his touch help me relax as he keeps going farther and farther until he bottoms out.

"Oh!" I gasp, as I wiggle my hips under his weight.

"Told you."

I've never felt so full in my life. Never did I think this is what my best friend was hiding all these years.

Breathing through the initial sting of being stretched and filled so completely, I cup Dax's cheeks and kiss him, letting him know it's okay to go.

He swivels his hips ever so softly, and it's all I need for that sting to go away and pleasure to once again take over every crevice of my body.

Dax's moves start slow then speed up. Each thrust of his hips stirs the need in my body for him.

I have never craved someone the way I crave this man right now. The way his hands know exactly how to tweak my nipples. The way his lips nip and suck on my neck. His hips thrust hard and fast, soft and slow. Every fiber of my being is a live wire ready to snap.

"You feel so damn good, Chloe. So fucking perfect," he growls. "All I want is to make you come again. Feel you come on my dick and make me explode."

"Yes. Oh God, yes!"

I drag my nails along his spine as I dig my heels into his ass, urging him on. His hips falter as he picks up the pace. With one last stroke of his finger over my clit, I'm done.

"Dax!" I shout as I start to come again. It's no less powerful than the first, but still rolls through my body as I feel Dax pour his own release into the condom.

He buries his head in my shoulder as he holds me through our release.

"Hell, that was amazing," he says into my neck.

"Perfect. It was perfect."

I don't know how much time has passed as our sticky bodies lie together, but I know one thing for certain.

I'm a goner for my best friend.

There was never any hope of doing anything but falling for Dax, and in one night, I've gone and fallen harder than I ever thought possible.

Chapter Twenty-Three

DAX

"How's Chloe doing with her first long road trip?" Marcus asks. "Doing okay?"

I nod. "I think it helps that the girls took her under their wing."

"Road trips aren't easy," he says, retaping his stick. "She'll be okay. She has good people around her."

"That and they're keeping her busy with jewelry orders."

I'm not sure I've ever seen Chloe as excited as when she told me they wanted custom jewelry made. She kissed me and then left me to study film on her couch while she went to work creating.

It was one of the best nights I've had in a long time. I prepped for our road trip these next two weeks—all against West Coast teams—while she worked on her designs, followed by a long night of orgasms.

Yeah, I could get used to that.

"Alright, everyone. That first period was good, but we need to work on our mistakes," Coach Andrews says. "It's still 0-0, but Vancouver is pushing us hard. Dax."

His eyes find me.

"Yes, Coach?"

"I'm putting you in with Marcus and Bode. I want to see you put it in the net."

"You got it."

Hell yeah. Finally a chance to start on the first line with these two guys. I try to model my game after these two. They're some of the best players—and guys—in the league.

"You've got this," Bode says, bumping his gloved fist against mine.

"Damn right," Marcus says. "Let's go shut this crowd up."

"On it," I fire back, as we all head out of the locker room.

From the moment the puck dropped, it's been nothing but an intense game. Vancouver's got the home crowd behind them. They're absolutely electric. Both teams have been fighting nonstop and we have nothing to show for it.

Getting moved up a line is big, and I don't want to screw this up as we take the ice for the beginning of the second period.

Marcus wins the face-off and shoots the puck over to Bode. Setting up, he skates back into our zone before sending the puck my way. Vancouver's defensemen are waiting for us. I deke around one of them and send the puck back to Marcus.

They're waiting for Marcus and crush him into the boards, but not before he gets the puck back over to me and I'm able to put it into the back of the net to score the first goal of the game.

"Fuck, yeah, Dax!" Bode piles on top of me as the lamp lights and the home crowd boos us. "That was awesome!"

"Keep doing that, Dax." Marcus smacks me on top of my helmet as I skate back to starting position for the puck drop.

Vancouver tries to match our goal, but we're ready. One goal fires up the team and we're all energized. Our defensemen stop the goal and shoot the puck my way. I take off. Not a single person from Vancouver is in my way.

Faking the goalie out, I fire the puck toward his stick side and the beautiful light flashes again.

"Breakaway goal. It's your night!" Marcus says, coming over to congratulate me.

"Great setup," I tell him.

"You made it look easy," Bode says.

"No goal is easy."

"That's about as easy as they come. Take the compliment." Marcus bumps me with his stick.

Vancouver is ready after this face-off and nabs the puck. For the rest of the second period, it's a battle of wills. They're a good team, as are we, and we're fighting to keep them off the scoreboard.

At the end of the second, one of their defensemen gets Noah tied up and they're able to put the biscuit in the basket.

"Damn it." I throw my water bottle down for the final shift change of the period as their fans celebrate the goal.

We run the clock out on the second period, then Coach Andrews goes over the game plan for the final period.

I'm staying with Marcus and Bode as he mixes up the second and third lines. Fresh legs to keep us on our feet the rest of the game.

Vancouver comes out swinging, but this time, Noah is there to stop a goal and sends the puck to me. Not able to get a breakaway this time, I send the puck flying to Bode who takes off across the ice and gets his own goal.

"Hell yeah, baby!" I skate up to him, jumping on top of him. "Great job!"

"Great assist!" He claps me on the helmet. "Keep it up, Dax."

The tide of the game is starting to lean in our favor. Vancouver is making silly mistakes that we're able to capitalize on. With one more goal late in the third, Vancouver pulls their goalie in favor of an extra man on the ice.

Coach sends us out to finish the game.

They're not giving in, playing hard and trying to get the puck away from us behind the net.

It slips out and I make my move. Cradling it in my stick, my skill is on point as I move it down the ice. With only one person in front of me, I send it flying.

Smack into the back of the net.

I thrust my arms in the air. A hat trick. I've never gotten one before in my life. I can't believe it.

"Fuck, yeah! We are going out to celebrate tonight!" Bode is grinning from ear to ear as he comes over to me. Marcus is waiting at the gate to welcome us back to the bench.

"Whatever Bode said, I agree with him."

"Even if it means going to a strip club?" I laugh.

"Doubt he said that," Marcus replies, smiling just as big as Bode.

"Great job, Fletcher." Coach congratulates me as I take my seat on the bench as the final minute of the game ticks away.

Knights win 4-2.

A line of reporters are waiting for us in the locker room before we can even hit the showers.

"You had a great game tonight. How does it feel to know your brother scored one more goal than you?" a reporter from one of the local news channels asks.

Way to be a buzzkill.

"Good for Duncan," I say, taking another swig of water. "I'm glad that I was able to help my team to a win tonight. Vancouver is a good team."

"Do you think those early goals helped you get the win?" he asks.

"It always helps to score first and get the momentum in your favor. Playing from behind is always hard."

"It helped get you that hat trick tonight with the empty net."

"I'm glad I was able to help my team win tonight," I say again.

What, just because it was an empty net goal, it doesn't count? I keep that to myself. I don't want to have a chat with the team PR. No, thanks.

"Hopefully next time we see you in Vancouver, our team is heading home with a win."

"See you next time."

At least the next person I talk to asks me about my hat trick. It helps bring back the excitement. I mean, they couldn't have waited to ask me a few questions before lobbing that question my way?

Of course on the best night of my career, Duncan has to do better. It's like I'm always in his shadow no matter what I do.

"Player of the game is Dax. Way to go." Coach tosses me a puck, as we all crowd in the visitors' locker room. "First hat trick of his career. Great job. Way to help seal the win for the team."

I nod in appreciation of getting the puck. "Thanks, Coach."

"We're leaving early tomorrow for Denver, and after that it's San Jose, Seattle, Anaheim, up to Edmonton, back to Vegas, and then home, so take it easy tonight. Eleven o'clock curfew. Got it?"

"Got it, Coach," we answer.

"You guys want to grab some beers and hang out in our room?" Bode asks.

"Sounds good to me."

Now that the adrenaline is starting to wear off, I could use a beer, a call with Chloe, and to hit the sack. Because I want to carry all this momentum forward.

It doesn't matter to me whether Duncan is doing better than I am or not. Because unlike him, I care about my team around me.

And I want to do everything I can to make sure we go far this season.

Chapter Twenty-Four

CHLOE

"I'm really glad you guys wanted to do this with me tonight."

Harper and Stevie look excited as I hold the door open.

"Are you kidding me? A night out and getting to try something new?" Harper asks. "I'm glad you suggested it."

"I never thought I'd want to try pole dancing, but it sounds fun," Stevie says.

"It was on my list of things to try, and I don't think Dax could do it with me."

"Your list of things?" Harper questions. "What's this list of things?"

"Things I wanted to do that Duncan didn't want me to try," I say. "A way to break out of my bubble and do everything I want to do."

"He sounds like my ex," Stevie says. "He wasn't the best guy."

"Yeah. I'm kind of over it. So I'm taking back control from him and doing everything I want to do."

"What else is on the list?"

"Break a world record, bungee jumping, go hot-air ballooning. A bunch of things."

"Okay, I love this idea, and I love that we get to help with pole dancing." Delight rings in Harper's voice.

After the gala, the three of us became fast friends. With the guys on their way home to Nashville after an early afternoon game in Vegas, the girls and I are spending a few hours together before they get home.

Checking in at the front desk of the dance studio, we're shown into a mirrored room with several poles extending from floor to ceiling. The lights are dim, but blue and pink bulbs color the room.

A few people are mingling about as the three of us find poles together. I unzip my jacket and adjust my sports bra that I paired with bike shorts. I have no idea what to expect, but did some research into best outfits to wear for beginners. Based on what Harper and Stevie are wearing, they did too.

"Welcome, everyone. I'm Jennifer, and this is our beginners class." A woman with short brown hair calls our attention to her. "We have some repeats tonight and some newbies in here, so I'm going to walk you through what we'll be doing." In high-waisted shorts and a sports bra, she looks the part of professional dancer.

I tighten my ponytail and hold on to my pole as I listen to her.

"We're going to start with a few basic spins to make sure you have your form right before progressing. After that, we'll go from there and you'll be a pro in no time."

She leaps onto the pole, climbing up it before holding on—with just her thighs—and spinning down it.

"Ow. How does that not hurt?" Harper whispers to us.

"Wow," someone else says.

"Don't worry." Jennifer laughs. "That's our advanced class. I've been training in the art of pole for years."

"I don't know if I'll ever be that good." A nervous laugh slips out.

"We're going to start by holding on to the pole." Jennifer grasps the bar overhead and grabs on in a kneeling position with her thighs. "Let's see if you can do this. I'll walk around to check your form and help adjust if you need it."

"I am definitely not strong enough for this." Harper tries to jump up and grab the bar, but slides off.

"Maybe don't try jumping?" Stevie asks, holding on for a few seconds before slipping off.

Reaching overhead, I grab the bar and pull my legs up and—oh damn, this is not easy. I do everything I can to squeeze my legs together around the bar but my arms can't hold me up.

"Why does this make my arms feel like they're noodles?" I shake them out as the instructor comes around.

"It's not as easy as it looks. You have to build up a lot of arm strength, but if you're committed, you'll get there." She helps each of us onto the pole and we hold it a bit longer this time, but nothing like her as she demonstrates it for us so we can try again.

"Did you see her shoulders?" I ask as she walks away.

"They are insane. No wonder she can do all these complicated moves," Stevie says.

"We have to come back. If only to get built like her." Harper points at each one of us. "I'm already having a blast and we've only been here for a few minutes."

I smile at the two of them. "Same. I'm so wrapped up in my jewelry that I forget I need to see actual people."

"Are you forgetting about Dax?" Stevie asks, a knowing look on her face.

"I couldn't if I tried. I hate that they've been on such a long road trip," I sigh.

"I'd say you get used to them," Harper starts, "but it's more that you fall into a rhythm. Video chats when you can, and lots of phone calls. It's harder on the kids."

"At least your kids can understand it. Poor Caleb just cries and cries when he wants Bode and he's not there. It breaks my heart." A sad look washes over Stevie's face. "But Caleb was happy as a bug when I left him with our grandmas, so tonight is about us."

"Yes. Thanks for coming with me to check this place out."

"Of course," Stevie says. "I'm with Harper. We have to come back."

Jennifer calls our attention back to her. "Okay. I'm going to show you two more moves and then I'm going to have you alternate on those. It will help build your strength so you can get more comfortable on the bar."

She walks us through the strong-hold grip—holding on to the bar with one leg in the air and tapping the other foot down, alternating them—and the pelvic tuck, moving both legs up and down.

None of the moves are easy as each of us work on them. I try to hold on to the bar as I lift my legs, but I'm bad. No matter how hard I try, I can't seem to hold on and move my legs.

"I think we're going to call it a night there." Jennifer claps her hands. "I know this isn't easy, but if you stick with it, I promise it will be worth it."

"My arms are gassed." I flop down onto the ground, not sure if I can move.

"I don't know if I'm going to be able to move tomorrow," Harper groans. "For real. Everything hurts."

"I don't know if I'll be able to lift Caleb into his crib

tonight," Stevie laments. "But I definitely want to come back."

"Me too." I grab my jacket and zip it up. "As much as it helped to take my mind off Dax, is it bad that I'm still anxious to see him when they get home?"

"No." Harper smiles at me as we walk out. "It means you picked one of the good ones."

"I think I did," I confess. "Sometimes I still worry because of what Duncan did, but—"

"I would not worry about Dax," Stevie says. "He looks at you like you are his moon. I've never seen two people so perfect and so sweet together."

I blush at her words. "He does not."

"I agree. It's the look of love." Harper nods. "And as someone who is told they are disgustingly in love, by my kids, I can confirm you two have the same kind of love."

I shake my head. "It's too early for love."

We haven't been together long at all; we couldn't possibly be in love, could we? I've known Dax my entire life. Could this be the next natural progression for the two of us?

I don't know what happens next, but I know I want to take it on with Dax.

Because with Dax by my side, everything will be okay.

Chapter Twenty-Five

DAX

DAX

Did you see Duncan has an exclusive interview on Really, Man? tonight?

MARCUS

What do you think it's about?

I have no idea

BODE

Should we be worried?

JASPER

Size small...really? Don't you think you're funny

NOAH

Umm, Jasper

BODE

Wrong text

GRAHAM

This text is discussing what Duncan's interview could be about

Yeah, what are you discussing?

BODE

Do we even want to know?

JASPER

You don't get to know

JASPER

So Duncan is giving an interview?

BODE

Now you're up to speed

JASPER

MARCUS

Assuming we're all going to watch it?

BODE

At least until Stevie gets home

MARCUS

Same. Harper should be home soon

How'd we beat them home?

BODE

Must mean their class is going well

NOAH

You guys have fun

GRAHAM

We're going to go have some fun of
our own

BODE

I'd say gross, but I'm assuming all of us are
doing the same thing

NOAH

Except Jasper

Ouch!

JASPER

Shows what you know...

MARCUS

Stop being cryptic

MARCUS

Are you seeing someone?

JASPER

...

BODE

Not an answer

JASPER

Don't care

JASPER

It's all you're getting

I fidget with the remote, a drink in hand, as I wait for the commercial to end and the new broadcast to start.

What in the world could Duncan be talking about on TV? Hell, who would give him the airtime?

When the familiar music of Sports Weekly News Network's most popular show starts, I sit up.

"Welcome to *Really, Man?* I'm Rhino Wellsley and I'm your host. Tonight, we have an exclusive interview with Detroit's newest star, Duncan Fletcher."

It cuts to footage of Duncan playing with Detroit. Damn it. He really is the better player out of the two of us. Even after a kickass stretch of games, it seems like no matter what I do, he's one-upping me.

It cuts to what looks like a pretaped segment on the set

of the show with the giant rhino logo stretched across the back of the studio. Duncan looks as smarmy as ever in a black shirt and his hair slicked back.

"Duncan, how has it been playing with Detroit?" Rhino asks him.
"It's been just the thing I needed after a hard summer, personally. The team has welcomed me with open arms this season."
"The summer you're referring to is your wedding that was called off?"
Duncan nods, a sad look coming over his face. "My fiancée ran off with my brother."
"Your brother, Dax Fletcher, star of the Nashville Knights?" he asks.

IT CUTS to footage of me playing, in case anyone doesn't know who I am.

"How did you take this blow?" Rhino asks.
"I was devastated. I mean, your fiancée and your brother cheating on you? It's a pain I wouldn't wish on my worst enemy."

"FUCK YOU, DUNCAN!" I turn the TV off and throw the remote. I can't stand to watch another minute of his lies.

DAX

> What the hell is the point of going on TV and lying?

BODE

> Fuck man, I'm sorry

MARCUS

Do you think something else is going on?

I have no idea

But why lie?

BODE

He probably still thinks he was the wronged
party

MARCUS

That fucker

I can't believe him

MARCUS

We'll settle it on the ice when they come
to town

BODE

That's diplomatic

Better than wanting to punch him in
the face

BODE

That would be really satisfying

MARCUS

Don't get benched before the game

Won't happen

I'm ready to kick their asses next week

MARCUS

Harper is home

MARCUS

See you guys later

BODE

So is Stevie

BODE

Don't let him ruin your night

HEARING THE GARAGE DOOR OPEN, I push every thought from my mind except the woman coming inside. I can tell Chloe about this later. Right now, I want to be with her in every way.

"Hi."

In a pair of bike shorts, flip-flops, and a jacket, she is a sight for sore eyes. I answer her with a hot kiss. I've missed this woman. After listening to the shit that Duncan is spewing about us, holding Chloe in my arms is the balm I need.

"Wow. I think you should always greet me like this." She bites down on her bottom lip. "Seriously, Dax. Wow."

I lift her into my arms and walk her so she's against the wall. "I've missed you."

She runs a finger along my jaw, sinking her fingers into my hair. "Not as much as I missed you."

"Did you have fun tonight?" I ask, kissing her neck and nibbling on the soft flesh there.

"Yes. We had a great time."

"I'm happy, but even happier that you're home."

"Just how happy?" she purrs.

"Care for me to show you?"

Chloe wiggles in my arms. "I could use a shower after class."

"Let me lead the way."

Damn. My dick is hard, already aching to be inside her. I am so far gone for this woman, it's not even funny. How can I be more in love with her now than I was before when I thought I couldn't love her more?

Maybe it's because I no longer have to hide my feelings for her. That she is returning them.

Leading her into the bathroom, I flip on the water in the shower and set her on the counter. I unzip her jacket and let it fall off her shoulders. Hard nipples poke through the flimsy material of her bra. I suck one into my mouth.

"Dax."

I love the way my name comes off her lips. The need and desire dripping from it.

"I can't wait to ravage you, Sunshine." I pull her shorts off and toss them behind me. "Clean every inch of your skin to get it all nice and dirty again."

"Do it, Dax. Please."

Steam fills the bathroom. Stepping back, I shuck off my clothes and do the same to her before carrying her into the shower.

Grabbing a glob of bodywash, I lather up my hands and run them all over her body.

"You're really going to make me wait?" she whines.

"I promise, it'll be worth it."

I dig my soapy fingers into her shoulders and she moans. "Okay, I think it will be."

I work my hands up and down her spine, massaging the muscles just above her ass. Her skin pinks in the hot water. Grabbing the shower attachment, I rinse off the soap. I take great care in concentrating on her clit.

"You are one mean, mean man."

I press a kiss to the tender skin on her hip. "Patience, Sunshine."

"Do you know how long I've been waiting for you?"

"I can only imagine."

I've been waiting a lot longer. I don't tell her that but stand and grab the shampoo to wash her hair.

I ghost featherlight kisses over her shoulder as I work

my fingers through her hair. "Can you do this all the time?"

I rinse out the soap as I pull her against me. "Okay."

I slide my free hand down her stomach and slip a finger inside of her.

"Finally."

Chloe grabs my hand as I move my fingers in and out of her. "Were you like this the whole time I was gone?"

"Yes. I missed you so much, Dax."

"Then hold on." I flip her around and drop to my knees. "Because you are going to come on my tongue first."

"First?" She pants as I throw her leg over my shoulder.

"Yes. Because I want to get you off before I take my time with you all night. Explore your body and have my way with you."

She sinks her fingers into my hair and grips tight as I slide my tongue inside her. She tastes so good, and the bite of pain spurs me on. I love how responsive Chloe is as her moans and groans hit my ears.

My dick is aching, damn needy to be inside this woman. I have to give myself a few strokes to stop myself from coming.

My knees hurt as I continue eating her out. Water sluices down her body between her breasts, dripping off her hard nipples.

She is so damn sexy, it hurts.

"I'm so close, Dax. Please."

"Please what?" I rock back onto my heels and strum my fingers over her clit.

"Please make me come."

I grin up at her. "Since you asked so nicely."

I suck her clit into my mouth and push three fingers inside her.

Chloe's body goes limp in my arms as she comes. I drink down every last drop of her release before she collapses onto the bench.

"That was…wow."

"Just wait, Chloe. I plan on doing that again. And again. And *again*."

I make good on my promise.

Chapter Twenty-Six

DAX

"I could get used to this."

Chloe burrows into my side as the sports channel plays quietly in the background.

"Get used to what?"

"Lazy mornings with you." She steals a strawberry from the bowl but I steal a kiss from her.

"Don't worry, there will be plenty more where this came from," I say.

"Too bad hockey is going to get in the way."

"Well, we've got a lot of hockey left to play."

Chloe's legs tangle with mine as we eat breakfast together on the couch.

"Well, on the non-hockey days, I want to get used to this."

"I can promise you that," I say, dropping a kiss on the crown of her head.

Is there anything better than being wrapped up with the person you love? One of these days, I'm going to tell her, but for right now, I'm happy with the way things are.

The doorbell rings, echoing off the app on my phone.

"Who's here?"

"I don't know." Grabbing my phone, I check the camera app, but it just spins as it tries to load, not showing who's on the screen. "Of course."

I drop the phone and hop off the couch. Swinging open the front door, my blood runs cold at the three people standing at my door.

Fuck.

This can't be happening. My parents are on my doorstep with Duncan right behind them.

Guess the team is in town already.

Mom looks shocked to see me opening the door in nothing but a pair of sweatpants. My dad is typing away on his phone, no doubt attending to some business, and Duncan looks like he'd rather be anywhere else.

"What are you guys doing here?" I ask in way of greeting.

"Is that any way to say hello to your family?" Mom chides, brushing past me to walk inside.

Fuck. This is the last thing I want right now.

"Is everything okay, Dax?" Chloe's voice calls out.

What am I going to do? Before I can say anything—before I can warn her—she bounds around the corner and comes to a dead stop when she sees who's standing here. In nothing but my T-shirt and a pair of shorts, it looks exactly like what we were doing. Spending the morning together after spending the night together.

"What the fuck? You really were cheating on me?" Duncan's voice is dead calm. I don't know if I've ever heard it like that.

I thought we'd have more time before Duncan learned that we were dating. Considering that I see him all of three days a year—two holidays and a random birthday—I didn't plan on being face-to-face with him so soon.

Seeing him in my entryway breathing fire, casting angry glances between me and Chloe?

Not how I saw my day going.

"So this is why you ran out on me?" Duncan huffs a breath.

"Do we really have to go over this again?" She's exasperated. "You were cheating on me."

"Clearly because you were cheating on me."

"That's not what happened," I interject.

"It doesn't look that way." Duncan crosses his arms, taking a step closer to me.

"Dax, do you care to explain exactly what is going on?" Dad asks. "Because your brother has a point here."

It figures they would take his side. They always have. It's why I've never really gotten along with my parents—hell, any of my family.

"I don't care what happened. Dax,"—Mom turns her attention to me—"you cannot be with this woman."

"Says who?"

My annoyance at their presence turns to anger. Who do they think they are, coming in here and telling me who I can or can't be with?

"Chloe left poor Duncan at the altar and ruined his life."

"Oh, is that what he said? In his big 'interview?'" Chloe spits out. Well, I'm guessing she saw that. No sense in hiding it.

"You're the one that is lying, Duncan." I take a step closer, but Dad steps between us. "Tell everyone else what they want to hear, what you want to believe, but we know the truth."

"You only know Chloe's truth."

"And I believe her." There is no doubt in my voice. Out

of everyone in this room, I would trust Chloe over all of them combined.

"What happened to the tramp?" Chloe crosses her arms over her chest, the hem of the T-shirt riding up ever so slightly.

Damn it, I wish we had more clothes on right now. Again, wasn't planning on my family showing up on my doorstep today.

"Chloe, is it really appropriate to be calling another woman that?"

"When she's sleeping with my fiancé, I can call her whatever I want."

I love that she doesn't back down from my mother.

"Dax Thomas Fletcher." Mom turns her ire to me. "It is obvious that you are the one that was cheating here. I cannot believe you would do that to your brother."

"Stop it!" Chloe snaps. "We were not doing anything behind Duncan's back. He was the one in the wrong here. Not us and I will not let you stand here and make us out to be the bad guys."

"Are you going to allow her to talk to us like that?" Dad asks.

I pull Chloe next to me. "It depends. Who do you believe?"

"This is a conversation that needs to be had when cooler heads will prevail," he says, the response not surprising.

"What, so they can get their stories straight?" Duncan throws a hand in our direction.

"Fuck off, Duncan. There's nothing to get straight because we're not lying about anything."

He eats up the distance between the two of us. He is a good head taller than I am. Another annoyance I have with my brother.

Taller. Better at hockey. He took to hockey like a fish to water whereas I had to work harder to get ahead.

"Fuck you, Dax."

"Get out."

"Are you going to treat us like this and kick us out of your house?" Mom looks stunned, appalled.

"Yes." I flit my gaze to her. "I am not going to sit here and let you treat the woman I love like this. Duncan is not the victim here, and if you believe him, then you're not welcome here."

"Dax." Chloe grabs my arm.

"No. You can leave," I say to them again.

"Seriously?" Duncan fires at me. "You're choosing her over us?"

"There was never a choice." I nod. "Now get out."

Mom storms out, Dad following behind her.

Duncan gets dangerously close, voice dropping low. "This isn't over."

And then he's gone.

"Fuck."

Chloe pulls me in for a hug, squeezing me hard.

"Did that really just happen?"

"Yeah."

She rests her chin in the center of my chest, staring up at me. She looks sick. "Are you really choosing me over your family?"

I tuck a loose strand of soft hair behind her ear. "There's no question, Chloe. I really didn't want to say it this way, but I love you. I've always loved you, and nothing Duncan or my parents say will change that. Truth is, I've loved you for as long as I can remember."

"Say it again."

"Which part?" I smile down at her, relief flooding my body.

"The part about you loving me."

"That's easy. I love you, Chloe Davis. And I will do everything in my power to protect you from whatever Duncan throws our way."

"Do you think it's going to get worse?"

I shrug a shoulder. "I don't know, but with him, you never know. I mean, I never expected him to blatantly lie on TV like that."

"So much for fact-checking." Chloe snorts. "You know, you could be with anyone. Why me?"

"It was never a question for me, Chloe. It was always you. I don't care what Duncan throws at us. I love *you*, Chloe."

"I love you too, Dax. I realize I was never in love before. Duncan gave me just enough to think it was love, but it wasn't. I know that now. Thanks to you."

I crush my lips to hers, a surge of happiness washing over me. I don't think I've ever been so happy in my life before. Hearing Chloe utter those words is everything I've always wanted.

No matter what happens, as long as it's the two of us, we can face it together. Face Duncan together.

I'm sure of it.

Chapter Twenty-Seven

DAX

NOAH

Are you going to be okay tonight?

DAX

Why wouldn't I be okay?

GRAHAM

Because your douche of a brother is
playing for Detroit now

I'll be fine

NOAH

Really?

NOAH

I wouldn't be

GRAHAM

Noah would love to punch his face in

NOAH

He cheated on my sister

NOAH

He deserves it

And he cheated on Chloe

But if anyone gets to punch him, it's me

MARCUS

There will be no punching of anyone tonight

BODE

You're no fun

JASPER

It's not like the man doesn't deserve it

NOAH

I know

NOAH

I said that

JASPER

Just confirming he does deserve it

MARCUS

And I want to win

MARCUS

We're looking good and I don't want anything to jeopardize our mentality this season

GRAHAM

You got it, Cap

NOAH

Ugh

NOAH

I hate how easily you agreed with him

GRAHAM

Usually you like it

NOAH

Yeah, when it's me

And we're off topic now

JASPER

Not surprised

And on that note, I want to check on Chloe before we leave

Make sure she's okay since Duncan will be there

NOAH

You're a better man than your brother ever was

Thanks, man

That means a lot

I set my phone down on the counter and scrub a hand down my face. I can't believe Detroit picked up Duncan. Since Coach Andrews came onto the scene, he's turned the team around. We're no longer the perennial losers we used to be. The same can't be said for Detroit.

Maybe that's why they picked up Duncan. He's a complete asshole off the ice, but on it?

I hate that no matter how well I play, I'm still in his shadow. Shouldn't being a good person count for more? Although based on his interview, you'd think I was the terrible person.

Me and Chloe.

"You okay?"

Chloe's voice pulls me from my thoughts.

Standing in my kitchen with her hair piled on top of

her head and face free of all makeup, she's never looked more beautiful to me.

"Worried about you."

"Me? Why?"

She hops up onto the counter next to me. A pen is twisted through her hair, holding it in place. I got a quick workout in while she was working on some new designs this morning.

"I don't want you having to run into Duncan again."

"Yeah." She lets out a long-suffering sigh. "I know."

"Are you going to be okay?"

"It's not like I'll have to see him tonight, right?"

"No." I push her legs apart and step between them, pulling her closer to me. "You can stay with Stevie and Harper in the family suite and head out right after. I can see you back—"

She slaps her hand over my mouth. "I can come see you after the game. It's not like I'll be hanging around down by the visitors' locker room."

"You sure?" I mumble against her fingers.

"Yes."

I tug her hand away and press a kiss to her palm. "I know, but I don't want you to have to deal with him again."

"Will *you* be okay?" Chloe asks. "You're the one that has to play against him."

"As long as he keeps his mouth shut, I should be fine."

Chloe waves her hand out in front of her. "So like fifty-fifty chance then."

"God, why is he such a dick? I mean really, what does he have to gain?"

"You're asking the wrong person. I don't know how the two of you are related."

"You're telling me."

"Look." Chloe wraps her arms around my shoulders. "Tonight will be fine. You'll ignore your brother, I'll stay with the girls so I don't run into your parents, and hopefully you won't catch any more flack about his damn interview."

I roll my eyes. "Poor Duncan, not being able to recover from you leaving him at the altar."

"I shouldn't laugh, but he really is the worst." Chloe hides her laughter in my neck. "Do you think you could get in some hits to him tonight? Nothing to get in the sin bin, but some cheap shots would be great."

"I'll see what I can do."

Chloe cups my cheeks, giving me a long, slow, sweet kiss. "I love you, Dax. Have I told you that lately?"

I smile against her lips. "Not since this morning."

"Well, I do. More than I ever thought I could love anyone."

"Yeah?"

She nods. "Yes. You're it for me, Dax. Just you."

I breathe her in. The faint tinny smell of jewelry making on her that never seems to go away with her citrus perfume. It's uniquely Chloe. Something that will always remind me of her.

My Chloe. My bright, shining light that brings more to my life than anyone else.

"Ditto."

Her laugh breaks the tension. "Ditto. I can't with you, Dax."

"It's a good thing you love me." I peck her nose. "At least half as much as I love you."

"Maybe even three-quarters."

"I'll take it."

Because I don't think I'll ever be able to quantify how

much I love this woman. There aren't enough words in the English language. They haven't been discovered yet.

Whatever it takes to protect Chloe, to make her happy, to show her I love her day in and day out, I'll do it. Because she's worth it.

And after what Duncan did to her, I will make sure she knows it every day.

Chapter Twenty-Eight

DAX

"**D**ax. I need a minute," Coach Andrews calls, disappearing into his office.

"What'd you do?" Noah asks, tugging his jersey on over his pads.

"Depends on who you ask."

I hang my jersey back up in my stall, not wanting to keep Coach waiting.

"You wanted to see me?" I ask, knocking on the door.

"Come in. Close the door."

"Did I do something?" I drop down into the chair across from him.

Getting called to the coach's office is the equivalent of going to the principal's office. I don't like the feeling one bit.

"Listen, I know there's a lot of heat with your brother right now, so I'm shifting the lines around tonight. You're going back to your old line for tonight."

"Wait, seriously?"

"Detroit is going to be gunning for you to protect

Duncan because of his interview. It's going to be a chippy game tonight."

"But it was all a lie!" I blurt out. "Why am I being punished when I did nothing wrong?"

"I have to do what is best for the team."

"Only for tonight?" I ask.

Marcus and Bode have been elevating my game ever since I was bumped up to first line. It's what I've been working toward and it feels great to see my hard work pay off.

This really fucking sucks.

"Just for tonight. I need cooler heads to prevail tonight, okay? Make sure the rest of the guys know it. I'm going to have a chat with Noah, too, if it makes you feel better."

Doubt he's getting dropped down a line, but he's also not on the first line.

"Okay."

"Play your game, Dax, and you'll do just fine tonight."

"Thanks, Coach."

Conversation over, I leave his office, but don't go right back to the locker room. I need a few deep breaths to get my head on straight.

I've done nothing wrong and Duncan keeps dragging me down with him. Now I'm losing my starting position? Damn, do I ever want to clock him.

But I can't. I don't want to prove Coach right by making this situation worse.

I need cooler heads to prevail.

If that's what Coach Andrews wants, that's what he'll get.

DAMN IT. The lamp lights up with another Detroit goal. We're down 4-1 now in the middle of the second period.

I hate that I'm not out there with Marcus and Bode, but it's like whatever good mojo we had going is gone.

"Change it up."

Hopping off the bench, I skate out to center ice for the puck drop. There's still plenty of time to turn things around, but I'm pissed.

Pissed that I'm not on my usual line. Pissed that we're not playing our best. And even more pissed that I'm staring down my brother across the ice now.

Exactly what Coach Andrews was trying to prevent.

"Looks like they finally let you on the ice. I didn't think they let shitty players out here," Duncan goads.

I ignore him, flying after the puck to grab it and hopefully close the gap. I shoot the puck to our winger who gets tied up with one of their defensemen, but going on the attack, I scoop it up and head toward the goal. Gauging where he's going to be in the briefest of seconds, I send the puck toward his glove side and it narrowly scrapes in.

"Hell yeah!" I throw my fist in the air.

Scoring doesn't shut him up. It's like wherever I am, he's right there—in my face shouting whatever comes to mind.

"Don't get used to that," Duncan chirps. "I'm not going to let you score again."

Ignore him.

Heading back to the face-off, Noah comes out onto the ice to replace one of our defensemen. Having played enough with him, it's nice to know he's out here. Especially with Duncan still chirping in my ear.

We win the face-off, but before I can get any movement toward their zone, Duncan is slamming me against the boards.

"How does it feel to know that everyone thinks *you're* the cheater?"

"Fuck off!" I elbow him in the pads and kick the puck out to Noah.

"I'm the golden boy now. Can't do anything wrong." He winks at me before taking off after Noah.

My jaw cracks as I grind my teeth together.

When did he become such an asshole? I don't know when it happened, but him acting like this is all I can remember.

Shaking my dickhead of a brother out of my head, I get back in the game. Noah blocks a shot Duncan takes and sends the puck my way.

Hell yeah.

Scooping it up, I take off. Our winger is skating side-by-side with me before Duncan comes up behind me for an illegal check.

"What the fuck?!" I yell from the ice.

The crowd is in an uproar as the refs miss it entirely.

"Poor baby, Dax. Not getting his way."

Anger is erupting inside me in full force as I pop off the ice and chase Duncan down. The last thing I want to do is let him score. Not while I'm on the ice.

I'm skating hard but Noah is with Duncan. He blocks the shot off his stick and sends it into the net.

With play whistled dead, the two of them get into it.

"He's not worth it," I tell Noah, pushing the two of them apart.

"He thinks he can get away with that shit?" Noah spits out.

"I already did, Fields. Get over it."

Noah bumps me out of the way, but I grab his elbow. "You know what Coach said."

"Aww. That's right. Skate back to your bench and get your leftovers," he says.

"Excuse me?" I drop Noah's arm and get in Duncan's face.

"You think you're better than me?" There's a sneer on his face. "You're not. You're not the better hockey player. You're not the better boyfriend or better person. You'll always be second place. Chloe's only using you to keep the bed warm until she decides she wants me back."

That's it. I can't take it anymore. I throw my stick on the ice and connect my gloved fist with Duncan's jaw.

Every thought flees my head as I pound my fists into my brother. An anger I've never felt is raging through me.

"You fucking dick. When did you become such an asshole?"

Duncan recovers and gets a few hits in, knocking me on my ass.

"Me?" Duncan spits blood from his mouth. "You're the one that came after me."

"Because you attacked Chloe!" I lunge at him again, but Noah holds me back.

"He's not worth it," Noah tries to tell me.

I break out of his arms and get one more punch in before it's the ref standing between the two of us.

Fuck.

Fuck.

I'm out of the game. Instigating a fight away from the play? That's a game misconduct penalty. I'll be lucky if I'm not suspended. It makes the hate burbling up inside of me grow, threatening to explode over the ice.

"You should listen to him." Duncan nods at Noah, goading me on. "Although I'm pretty sure his sister might be worse than Chloe."

And now it's Graham holding Noah back.

"You couldn't have kept it together?" Bode is escorting me off the ice.

"You should have heard what he was saying—"

"He was doing it to get under your skin and now you're ejected."

"Fuck."

"Yeah. You're going to get your ass chewed out after the game."

Don't I know it. I deserve it.

"I really hate him," I tell Bode as Graham hands me my stick and gloves.

"We'll try to win to shut him up, but you need to cool off, Dax," Bode says.

One of the assistant coaches escorts me back to the locker room. I'm still fuming as I chuck my helmet into my locker. A TV plays the game in the corner, but I can't concentrate.

I'm mad at Duncan for his shit. I'm mad that I lost my cool. I'm mad that I'm not out there helping my team.

I'm mostly mad at Duncan because he started all of this, but I can't believe I let him get to me.

"Maybe I am just as bad as he is," I say to no one in particular.

"You're not."

Spinning on my skate, Chloe is standing in the locker room.

"How'd you get down here?"

In my jersey and a pair of jeans, she looks worried as she twists the end of one of her braided pigtails.

"Harper helped me."

I scrub a hand down my face. "I really fucked up, Sunshine."

"I know. But you're not like him."

I drop down onto my chair. "Are you sure? How do you know?"

Chloe closes the distance and drops down onto my lap. "Because I know you. I have some idea of what Duncan said."

"He said—"

She claps her hand over my mouth. "I don't need to hear it. I'm sorry he got to you."

I bury my head in her neck, breathing her in. "I'm sorry. I was trying to be the bigger person but he just kept pushing."

"He has a tendency to do that."

"I'll be lucky if I'm not suspended."

Chloe cups my cheek, rubbing her thumb along my jaw. "I thought that was hard to do?"

"I guess when I screw up, I go big. It wasn't during play and I instigated it. Just reiterates what Duncan said—that I'm the bad guy."

"Does it help that I know you're not the bad guy?" She smiles at me.

"Yes." I blow out a breath, some of the anger starting to cool. "I wish I wasn't related to him."

"I don't."

"You don't?"

She shakes her head. "Do you think we'd be here otherwise?"

"Maybe."

"We can't change that he's your brother, but maybe tomorrow we take a day. Just the two of us. Put Duncan out of our heads. No hockey. No lists. You and me."

"That sounds pretty good."

Cheers echo from the arena. Looking up at the TV, I see that Marcus scored, bringing us within one. At least they're still playing well without me.

"I'm going to go get cleaned up. I'll meet you in the family suite down here?"

"Or…" Chloe stands up.

"Or what?"

She looks up at the TV. "There's about ten minutes left, right?"

I look up, nodding to confirm she's right. "What are you getting at?"

"Think there's time for a quick blow job in the shower?"

I don't think I've ever heard her utter those words, but I'm not going to say no right now. Stripping out of my pads as quickly as I can, I follow Chloe into the showers.

Yeah, this is not what I should be doing right now, but I really don't care. This is exactly what I need to put my shitty performance out of my head.

Flipping on the water, I let it run over my body as my dick hardens at the sight of Chloe, still fully dressed, dropping almost to her knees and wrapping her hand around me.

"I think this will help." She gives me a long slow stroke.

"What has gotten into you?" I groan, throwing my head back, doing my best to block the water from hitting her.

"What can I say? Boring Chloe left the building."

She wraps her lips around the head and sucks. Holy fuck, that feels so damn good. Seeing Chloe like this is a sight to behold.

Between her tongue and hand, she knows exactly how to get me off. Sliding off, she drags her finger along the throbbing vein.

"We really don't have time to play," I say.

"We have some time." She places hot, open-mouthed

kisses along the hard flesh before swirling her tongue around my leaking head.

Her mouth is stretched wide around me as she bobs up and down. God, I wish I had time to strip her down and fuck her senseless in here, but I know there isn't time for that.

I'll take what I can get right now.

"You need to wrap it up, Sunshine."

Taking a deep breath, she sucks me as far as she can. I bump the back of her throat as she squeezes my balls.

"Yessss," I hiss. "I'm going to come."

She holds me to the back of her throat and I hold on to the shower stall as I come. Fuck, it feels so damn good to empty my release into her mouth.

Steam and heat swirl around us as she pops off me, wiping the spit and cum that gathered at the corners of her mouth. Water droplets cling to her hair and her mouth looks thoroughly fucked.

"Feel better?" she asks.

"Yes."

"Good." Chloe pecks me on the corner of my mouth. "Now, I'll meet you in the family room after the game. Go watch the rest of the game in the locker room and I'll be waiting for you."

Watching her stalk off, there's a confident sway to her ass.

I can't believe that woman is mine. I have no idea what is going to happen after this game, but at least one thing in my life is uncomplicated.

And that's Chloe.

Chapter Twenty-Nine

CHLOE

"You know, you didn't have to do something off my list," I say. "Especially since you don't like heights."

Dax burrows in closer behind me. "I wanted to. This was the best thing I could think of to get away from everything that is happening."

"I still think it's unfair you got a two-game suspension. I mean, how many players fight during the game and nothing happens?"

"It's because play wasn't going on," he tells me, not for the first time.

"I hate that you got suspended, but he deserved it."

I still don't know what Duncan said, but I can only imagine. Dax is the most even-keeled person I know. He hardly cusses and is always one to tell you how he feels. He doesn't react.

For him to have done that? I can fill in the gaps as to what Duncan said.

"It is what it is."

"At least Duncan has a gnarly bruise."

Dax laughs behind me as a blue and yellow balloon is

unfurled in front of us. The sun isn't even up yet as the two of us wait for our hot-air balloon ride.

Dax found a place outside of the city. Waking up far too early, with mugs of coffee in hand, we made the drive, wanting time for the two of us.

"Does it make you feel better that he didn't give me one?"

"Yes." I lean back and kiss him on the jaw.

"You two ready?" the balloon pilot asks. A stocking cap covers his head and a jacket is zipped up to his chin. There's a bite to the air this morning.

"Yes."

He goes over a quick safety brief before we climb into the basket. The crank of the fire filling the balloon takes over as we lift off the ground. The field and the trucks below us get tinier and tinier as we float into the sky.

I shift behind Dax, whose knuckles are turning white on the rim of the basket.

"I've got you."

Squeezing my front to his back, I peer out around his arm to see the city sprawling out beneath us.

"It's not that bad."

"Do you want to let go?" I ask.

"No," he answers immediately, although one hand clings to my forearm.

"I won't let anything happen to you."

With just the sound of the burner going, it's peaceful this high. We move up and down, following the river.

"I find myself doing lots of new things with you lately, Sunshine."

"What's your favorite?" I ask.

"Do you really have to ask?" He looks over his shoulder at me.

"Let's not say that one out loud," I whisper, looking at

the pilot of the balloon behind us. He doesn't need to know what we're both thinking. "Give me your second favorite."

"I'd have to say zip-lining."

"Does this mean you're starting to like heights?"

He shakes his head. "No. But I liked getting to do it with you."

"It was quite nice to feel you wrapped around me."

"Kind of like right now."

His body shakes with laughter. "We really shouldn't keep going down this train of thought."

"You're right. Can I tell you my favorite memory of us then?"

"Do I know this?"

"No. It was after your grandpa broke his leg and you were out of school helping him."

"You bringing me my homework is your favorite memory?"

I swat his chest. "It was after he moved back home when he was better. We went canoeing that day in the mountains."

"It was hot as hell and we forgot the cooler in the car."

I nod. "We had nothing and were dying of heat and finally jumped in the river and ended up losing one of the paddles."

"I'm glad you didn't put canoeing on your list," Dax says. "I'd do it with you, but I wouldn't be happy."

"Oar or not, that was one of my favorite days. We didn't have a care in the world back then."

"I think my only worry was if you liked me."

"I happen to like you now," I say, resting my chin in the center of his chest. "A lot."

"Ditto."

I snuggle into his chest as he drops a kiss to my head.

With the two of us up here, it feels like we're in our own bubble. That the rest of the world won't touch us.

As soon as we land, all of our problems will still be there.

Dax's suspension.

Duncan and his vitriol.

No one said love is easy, but I wish it wouldn't be this hard.

But if this is what it means to be with Dax, I'll take it. I've never felt so loved or so wanted as I do when I'm with Dax.

How can one person make you realize everything you've been missing in your life?

Whatever comes next, I'll do anything to protect what Dax and I have.

Because it's worth *everything*.

Chapter Thirty

CHLOE

DAX

Have fun watching the game tonight

CHLOE

Ditto

That's just mean

Sorry

You set me up for it

I still love you

Yeah, yeah 🙄

I hate that I can't be out there tonight

Last one and then you'll be helping your team

Back on my old line

Coach Andrews knows you're sorry

You'll get back up there with Marcus and Bode

I know you will

I hope so

All because I couldn't keep it together

Duncan will get his due

You think?

Doesn't he always?

Maybe then your parents will be on our side

Maybe...

Harper's here

I know you want to be out there, but keep your chin up and cheer on your team

I love you

Ditto

"Hey." I swing open the front door to a grinning Harper.

"Hi." She gives me a hug before walking inside. In a pair of leggings and an oversized Knights sweatshirt, she's ready to cheer the guys on.

"Thanks for coming over tonight."

"It's been a long week. I need a girls' night," she says, toeing out of her shoes. "I wish Stevie could have come."

"Too bad the game landed on bridge night for their grandmas."

"Next time." Harper holds up a bottle of wine. "Want a glass?"

"God, yes."

I grab one of the waiting glasses next to my cheese board on the coffee table and pour us each a glass.

"How are you doing with everything?"

We drop down onto the sofa as the game against Boston starts.

"I'm worried."

"About Dax?"

I nod, grabbing a cracker and pepperoni slice and popping it in my mouth. "Yes. I think this whole thing with Duncan is affecting him more than he's letting on."

"Have you talked to him about it?"

"I've tried, but I don't think he wants me to worry."

"Which only makes you worry more," Harper confirms. "These men sometimes."

"Dax is usually up-front with how he feels, but I think it's a sticky situation."

"Because you were once engaged to said brother."

"Exactly."

"I'm assuming you saw the post-game interview with Duncan?" Harper asks.

"Ugh. Could he be hamming it up any more? *Having my brother come after me after he stole my fiancée?* I can't believe I ever fell for him."

"We've all been taken by a pretty face," Harper says. "I know I have."

"What happened with that?" I ask, sipping my wine.

"Oh, I never got rid of him." She grins back at me, laughing. "Marcus is more than a pretty face. I'm head over heels for him."

The horn sounds and our attention turns back to the game. The guys are swarming Marcus as the Knights take an early lead.

"And a talented hockey player too." I nudge her with my toe.

"Yeah, he's pretty great." She's beaming. "Do you think Duncan is going to leave you two alone?"

"I don't know. I can't figure out why he's doing this. I mean, is this why he got picked up by Detroit? They felt bad for him and he's playing it up so they keep him on the team?"

"It's annoying he has the game to back up the talk." Harper winces. "I hate to say it, but he's a good player."

"And no matter how well Dax plays, Duncan is always overshadowing him, and I hate it. He gets a hat trick and they ask about his brother scoring four goals that night."

"I wanted to smack that reporter," Harper laments. "Let him have his moment. You only get one first hat trick."

"Right? They're making it worse. Sometimes I think…"

"What?" Harper mutes the game and rests her elbow on the back of the couch. "What are you thinking?"

"That maybe if Dax and I weren't together, Duncan would go away."

"Do you want that?"

"God, no. It would probably make things easier, but I'm tired of Dax taking the brunt of Duncan's revenge."

"Would a statement from the team help?" she asks, munching on a piece of white cheddar.

"Dax talked to the PR team and they said it would come down to a he said, she said kind of thing and it'd drag us further into the mud."

"Well, based on everything I know about Duncan,"

Harper says, "he's going to do something to fuck up again. He just can't help himself."

"Well, here's hoping it's sooner rather than later. Because if I can't launch my business because of him, I'm going to be pissed. I can see him complaining about me to press to get them on his side and people not coming to my store."

"Does that mean you're closer to finding a storefront?"

I nod. "I've been looking at a few spots near Broadway. I figure that's the best way to get foot traffic."

"Love that idea. Do you want any help looking at them? I can go with you."

I smile back at her. "Once I find some, I'll let you know. I know Dax wants to come with me."

"Of course he does." Harper wiggles her fingers in front of me. "Did you notice?"

"Oh my God!" I set my wine down and grab her hand. "You're wearing it."

"I love it. So do the girls."

I look at the silver ring with three gemstones—one for each of their kids. It took me longer than I thought to make it because I wanted it to be perfect. I mean, I want every piece to be perfect, but for a friend? I didn't want to embarrass myself and give her something that was subpar.

"It looks great."

"I love it. And you've got some interested parties at school who might want a custom ring too."

"Really?"

She nods. "Yes. You're talented, Chloe. Don't let others get in your head about it. You've got what it takes."

"That makes me happy to hear. I really want to do this."

"You will. I know it."

"Now you sound like Dax." I laugh.

"Great minds think alike."

The rest of the game goes by in a blur of wine, cheese and crackers, and a Knights win. I breathe a sigh of relief that the Knights came out on top of their last two games without Dax. It would've made it worse for Dax if they hadn't. He would have carried that weight on his shoulders.

"Thank God they won."

"Dax is in the clear." Harper knows exactly what I'm talking about.

"I know he's ready to get back out there."

Harper grabs the empty tray and her glass and carries them into the kitchen. "Be honest. That had to have felt good for Dax, right?"

I hold my thumb and finger a smidge apart. "Just a little. Dax won't admit it, but I know it did."

"I bet." Harper wraps me in a hug. "I know things might seem hard now, but just know that they'll get better. I promise. As long as you and Dax stick together, you'll be okay."

I squeeze her back harder. "Thanks, Harper. You're a good friend."

"I'm glad Dax has you and that we get to have you now too."

"Thanks."

"I'll see you at the next home game."

"Bye."

I close the door behind her. It's like the weight that's been resting on my shoulders has lifted. It's been hard dealing with Duncan and all his lies.

Having people like Harper in my corner makes it easier to navigate. With them by our side, hopefully Dax and I can come through the other side.

Sooner rather than later.

Chapter Thirty-One

DAX

"That was a great game, gentlemen." Coach Andrews is standing in the locker room, looking at all of us. "I'm proud of the way we're playing. We've got a tough stretch of games coming up and I want all of us locked in. We'll do a light practice before heading to Tampa for our last game down here."

"Thanks, Coach," everyone echoes.

He heads back to his temporary office as guys hit the showers. I drop down onto the bench, stretching my legs out in front of me.

"That was a good game from you," Marcus tells me.

"Thanks." I grab my bag, waiting for the others to head out to the team bus that will take us back to the hotel.

"I know you're not back out there with us on the first line, but you're still playing for the team and that's something Duncan would never do."

"Got that right," Noah agrees. "Did you see Detroit got crushed this afternoon?"

"You don't have to sound *so* happy about it," Graham says.

"Sorry." Noah smiles. "I can't help it. I hate Duncan and he deserves it."

"Yeah, I agree," Jasper says. He's not paying attention, tapping away on his phone.

"Do you think we could win the Stanley Cup and he would notice?" Noah asks, nudging Graham as we all head to the bus.

"Right now? No."

We file onto the bus and head back to the hotel north of Miami.

"You guys want to get a drink before we hit the sack?" Bode asks.

"I'm game," I say.

"We're in." Noah and Graham drop into the seats behind me and Bode.

"I'm going to call Harper and check in on the kids and I'll be there," Marcus says.

It's a quick trip back to the hotel at this late hour without much traffic. Marcus and Jasper head upstairs while Bode, Noah, Graham, and I head for the bar.

"Want to do a pitcher of beer?" Bode asks.

"Sure. I'll get the first round."

I order our drinks as highlights from tonight's games play on the screen. Drinks are handed over without any comment as to who he is serving. Thank God, because I don't want to deal with people tonight.

"Thanks, man."

Bode takes the glasses and passes them around as I pour.

"You know, we still haven't cashed in on our bowling win," Jasper says.

"Does this count?" I ask.

"Fuck, no. We have to do something fun," he says.

"Glad to know drinks with your boys isn't fun," Graham says.

"This is just what I need after that game." Bode kicks his legs out at the high-top table we're all crowded around. "I'm ready to get home and sleep in my own bed."

"Same. I miss Chloe," I say.

Not that we spend every night together, but I've gotten used to seeing her whenever I want. This is the worst part about being a professional hockey player. Being gone for days, sometimes weeks, at a time and only having video calls, the phone, and texts to communicate.

I don't care if it makes me a sap, but I can't wait to get home and just hold her in my arms. It's been a hard few weeks, and she's the only thing that's making it worth it.

"One more game," Jasper says. "I think we can all make it one more game."

"Are you going to tell us what's been going on with you?" Noah asks. "Seriously, we tell each other everything."

"Don't I know it." Jasper laughs.

"You say that like it's a bad thing," Graham prods.

"Did we really need to know that Dax and Chloe went to a sex club?" He quirks a brow at Noah and Graham.

"Probably not, but hey, it got the ball rolling for them to get together. I'd say we had a big part of that," Noah says proudly.

"You want to take credit for my relationship?" I sip on my beer. Damn, that really is refreshing after tonight's game.

"At least some part of it," Noah reiterates.

"Eh. If you want to, I don't care," I say.

"Dax did the hard part." Bode squeezes my shoulder. "You had a conversation. Like an adult. Something a lot of people don't know how to do."

He swings his gaze to Jasper.

"Ugh. Not back to me again," he whines.

"Then tell us what we want to know," Bode almost shouts at him. "You've been keeping a secret and we want to know."

A voice from the TV snags our attention. "Next on *Really, Man?* we have breaking news out of Detroit. Stay tuned for news on Duncan Fletcher with your host Rhino Wellsley."

An image of Duncan being hauled away in cuffs flashes across the screen.

"Wait, turn that up," I call out to the bartender.

"Was he in cuffs?" Marcus asks, his jaw dropping.

"He said *Duncan* Fletcher, right?" Noah asks.

I smack him on the shoulder. "Obviously I'm sitting right next to you."

"I wanted to make sure there wasn't some other Fletcher we were getting him mixed up with. He was getting arrested?" Noah looks giddy. Out of all the guys here, he probably hates him as much as I do for the way he treated his sister.

"Shh!" I shush them as the intro music comes on.

"I'm Rhino Wellsley, and welcome to *Really, Man?* Thanks for joining us tonight. In a sting earlier this evening, Detroit hockey stars Duncan Fletcher and Chad Orman were arrested after being implicated in an illegal gambling ring. Dozens were arrested as Detroit police were on scene after an anonymous source tipped them off. While we don't know everything that's going on, we have received word that documents show that both players allegedly threw games in order to win bets. Really, man?" Rhino asks. "Detroit is at the bottom of the league and you couldn't try to win in your favor?"

A video is now playing of Duncan shouting at the camera as he's being hauled away in a police car.

"I've been under a lot of stress. It's not my fault!" he cries.

"Holy shit," I mutter.

"We'll have more as news breaks, but I've been doing some digging into both players."

Images of Duncan and Chad's social media accounts come up on the screen. Parties. Women. Nothing even remotely related to hockey.

Rhino points at the images. "Now, these aren't their 'official' accounts. We had to go digging to find these, but it looks like Duncan has been partying with women for the last few years. And for those that don't remember, he gave an interview about his fiancée cheating on him. Really? Really? It looks like he rubbed off on his teammate, because these two have been doing nothing but partying and making the rounds through Detroit. Really?"

"We need shots." Bode darts over to the bar and orders them for us.

"I can't believe this."

Shock doesn't even begin to cover it. Was Duncan trying to get in the team's good graces because *this* is what he was doing off the ice?

A shot is pushed into my hand and I take it without thinking.

Why the hell have I been so worried about breaking out of Duncan's shadow when that's the kind of person he is? I know I'm a good player and an even better man.

"You know, when I was hoping Duncan would get what was coming to him, this isn't what I had in mind," Noah says.

"Betting against your team?" I shake my head. "I mean, who does that?"

My phone buzzes in my pocket and I pull it out as the guys continue discussing the news.

CHLOE

Are you seeing this?

DAX

I can't believe it

Me either

Betting against the team?

God, what a dick

Seriously

Who does that

Does this mean we're done with him?

I hope so

I'm going to reach out and see if he needs anything

This is why I love you

OPENING A NEW TEXT THREAD, I type in Duncan's name and fire off a message.

DAX

Look, I know we don't always see eye to
eye on a lot of things, but if you need
anything, I'm here for you

DUNCAN

Fuck you

If you weren't such a damn Goody Two-
shoes, I wouldn't be in this situation

How the hell is this my fault?

If I didn't have to live up to your name, I'd
be fine

Sorry, this is all you

You're the big brother and the family
favorite

I'm not taking the heat about this for you

Then fuck off

I've tried to be the bigger person, Duncan,
but I'm done

Done with the way you treat me, treat Chloe

I'm over it

If you really need my help, I'm here for you,
but it doesn't seem like you do

I FLIP my phone around and show the guys what Duncan
said.

"What a fucking asshole," Jasper says. "He thinks this is

because of you? What warped sense of self does he have that you're the cause of all of his problems?"

"I don't know, but if this means I'm done, I can't complain."

"Still sucks to lose a brother," Marcus says.

I shake my head. "I have you guys. That's all that matters."

"Aww." Noah leans over, giving me a noogie. "You love us."

"Get off." I push him off of me. "Are you twelve?"

Marcus tips his beer in our direction. "This is what you get when you say we're your brothers."

"I regret it already."

"No, you don't. You love us," Bode says. "We love you too."

"Aren't you guys supposed to be hockey players?" The bartender comes up from behind us, startling me.

"We're in touch with our feelings. You should try it," Jasper bites out.

He rolls his eyes. "Last call. Need anything?"

"One more round of shots," I say.

The ticker at the bottom of the screen has news of Duncan's arrest flying across as the lead headline between the night's scores.

I hate to feel a sense of relief at my brother's downfall, but now it seems like my life is finally my own.

Mine *and* Chloe's.

No more living in Duncan's shadow. Having to worry about what he'll say or do that will affect us.

I don't know how my parents will feel about this, but I'm sure they'll be on Duncan's side and blame me like he did.

I don't care. I have Chloe. Chloe is all I need. I have Chloe, these guys that have become my family, and hockey.

Now I need to make sure that Chloe gets her dream.
Charms by Chloe.
I'll make it happen if it's the last thing I do.

Chapter Thirty-Two

CHLOE

DAX

Meet me downtown today

CHLOE

Cryptic much?

I have a surprise for you

Just go with it

Really?

There've been too many surprises lately

I promise, this should be a good one

Trust me

I always do

I stare at the address in our texts again, wondering what in the world is going on. It's been a week since I last saw Dax. It's been a week since I last saw Dax. After a short stint at home, he's been away with the Knights on an East Coast road trip. We talked every day, but it wasn't the same as seeing him. At least it gave me time to stock up on rings and my newest bracelet design. I've perfected the bracelets and can't wait to add them to my online shop.

"I think this is it, ma'am."

The only reason I know it's the right spot is Dax is standing outside in a sweatshirt and a red Knights hat pulled low over his eyes as passersby walk past, ignoring him.

"Thank you."

I step out of the car, waiting as a bachelorette party stumbles past.

"Hey." Dax smiles at me.

My heart flutters in my chest. It feels like a lifetime since I last saw him. With all the drama with Duncan and him being gone, there's so much we need to talk about. But that can wait until later.

"Why'd you ask me to meet you down here?" Resting my hands on his chest, I drop a kiss on his cheek as he wraps his arms around me.

"Like I told you earlier, I have a surprise for you."

"It's only because it's a surprise from you that I'm amenable to it."

"Good. Then I need to blindfold you for it."

"Okay, is this a sex club thing? Are we going back?"

Dax laughs, spinning me around. "Not quite."

"Then what are we doing?"

He ties the material over my eyes. "Where's your sense of excitement, Chloe?"

"Fine." I cross my arms over my chest as Dax turns me

in the opposite direction. "You know, someone might think you're kidnapping me."

"We're going maybe fifty feet. I don't think anyone is going to pay attention to us."

"Just as well. Probably not even the weirdest thing that people will see out here tonight."

"You got that right."

Dax steers me farther away from the noise and chaos of Broadway. It's not more than thirty seconds before he stops. There's a small jingling and a door opening.

"Where are we?"

"Just wait," he reiterates.

Wherever we are, it's cool and smells stale. The lock clicks behind me as a brightness hits my eyes through the soft material.

"Ready."

Deft fingers undo the bandanna and pull it away. It takes a second for my eyes to adjust to the light, but when they do, I see I'm standing inside what looks to be an old store. Exposed brick walls line three sides, while windows, covered with craft paper, face the street. There's a small counter at the back and a table sitting in the middle, but other than that, it's completely bare.

"Dax. What is this place?" I spin around, facing him, slipping out of my jacket.

"Well, I'm hoping it might be the new storefront for Charms by Chloe."

"Wait, what?"

I look around again. Old, fluorescent lights flicker from the high ceilings. A love song filters in from one of the nearby bars.

"This is…" I don't even know what to say. A storefront for my business? "How did you find this place?"

Dax smiles at me. "I found a realtor a few weeks ago. I

didn't think we could get in and see this place for a few more weeks, but an opening came up and I took it. It's yours."

"Wait, seriously?" The hardwood floors creak underneath my feet as I move toward Dax. "I don't know what to say."

"Look, if you don't like it, we've only lost out on rent and a security deposit." He rubs a nervous hand over the back of his neck. "I know you want to do this on your own, so the lease is for a year, and I only paid the first three months. I figured you'd yell at me if I paid for the whole year up front."

"You figured correctly." I rest my fisted hands on my hips.

"I know you have some money saved up already from selling online and I know you want to do it yourself, but a little help doesn't hurt. Not when you and I are trying to start our own lives together."

"Our own lives, huh?"

Dax wraps his arms around me. "I've been trying to think of a way to show you that we can be together on our own, free from all the drama of Duncan."

I roll my eyes. I still can't believe he is caught up in illegal gambling and throwing games. I never thought he would stoop so low. And when they showed all the women he was with? I wasn't surprised at all. He finally got what he had coming to him when they started speaking up about what a douchebag he is.

It's what Dax and I have known since the beginning, yet no one wanted to believe us. The cherry on top? Duncan was banned from the league.

"You really got this for me?" I ask again, trying to wrap my head around it.

"Yes. I want your dream to come true. I don't care

that my parents think what happened to Duncan is my fault. We know the truth. As long as I have you, I have everything I need. You can check off the last item on your list, I get to be with you, and hopefully bring The Cup home."

"Dax." Emotion chokes my voice.

"I have one more surprise."

"More than this?"

Dax clears his throat and pulls a piece of paper from his pocket.

BLONDE HAIR, BLUE EYES, EASY SMILE, MY BEST FRIEND

You CREATE THE CHARMS, BUT YOU'RE THE CHARMER

You WANT TO BE SPICY MUSTARD, BUT YOU'RE YELLOW

BUT THAT'S OKAY, CAUSE I THINK YOU'RE SPICY

You WANT TO TRY ANYTHING AND EVERYTHING

EVEN IF IT SCARES YOU AND ME

AND I DON'T CARE IF YOU NEVER WANT TO MARRY

BECAUSE TO ME, YOU'RE PERFECT

BORING YELLOW MUSTARD AND ALL

So DON'T TRY TO CHANGE AND BE SPICY

BECAUSE I LOVE YOU THE WAY YOU ARE

AND NO MATTER WHAT HAPPENS

IT WILL ALWAYS BE THE TWO OF US TOGETHER

I LOVE YOU, CHLOE. I LOVE YOU, FOREVER.

"YOU WROTE ME A POEM?" Tears spill over my eyes.

"I was trying to be Shakespeare. He's the epitome of romance."

"He is."

"I don't think I got it quite right. There were a lot of rules and I figured what the hell, just write it."

"It's perfect, Dax." I shake my head. "Shakespeare couldn't have done better if he tried."

I pull the paper from his hand to see it. Little dots pepper the edges. No doubt from him trying to brainstorm ideas and tapping his pen on the paper. A few lines are crossed out.

"I want you, Chloe. I want us to break away from all the expectations we've put on ourselves to be better than people who don't care about us."

"I want to be just us. If our families and friends can't accept that, then we'll deal with it. I love you, Dax."

He grins down at me. "Ditto."

Then he seals his mouth over mine. Every thought flees my mind as my need for Dax takes over. It's been too long since I've been with him.

And all I want is him.

I sink my fingers into his back, urging him on as our tongues fight for control of this kiss. He hefts me into his arms, carrying me across the room before setting me down on the counter.

I can't contain my need for this man. Grabbing the hem of his sweatshirt, I pull it up and over his head. He wastes no time yanking my tank up and off.

My hard nipples brush against the muscles in his chest and I gasp. It's been too long without his touch. Warmth spreads through me as his fingers undo the buttons on my jeans.

"Please, Dax. I need you now."

"You've got me, Sunshine. I'm almost there. Lift up."

I do as he says, Dax shimmying my jeans over my hips and butt. Pulling my underwear to the side, he sinks his finger inside my dripping pussy.

"Gah!" My shout echoes around the empty space. "So good, Dax."

"I love how wet I can make you."

"Only you," I purr.

Dax curls his finger inside me as his mouth trails warm kisses down my neck, nibbling on the tight buds of my nipples through the cotton fabric.

I comb my fingers through his hair, holding on tight as he lavishes me with attention. It's everything I need.

"Are you going to come on my fingers?" Dax asks, pushing two fingers inside me. "Or do you want to come on my cock?"

"Cock. Now," I demand.

"Whatever you want, Chloe, you'll get. Always."

Stepping back, Dax pulls his wallet from his back pocket and tosses it on the counter next to me before pulling his dick out.

He gives it a long, slow stroke that has my mouth watering. I grab his wallet and fish out the condom and toss it at him. His eyes lock on mine as he tears it open and slides it down his hard length.

Dax prowls to me and drags himself through my wet pussy. It's a tease, meant to torment. I can't wait. Taking him in hand, I line him up and push him inside.

"Fuck," he bites out. "Why do you always feel so damn perfect, Sunshine?"

"Not nearly as good as you make me feel."

Swiveling his hips, he starts to move. Resting on my elbows, I relish each thrust of his hips. The feeling of him spreading me wide open.

Each pump of his hips pushes me that much closer to

exploding. Every nerve ending is on fire. My toes curl as my eyelids flutter closed. Dax licks and sucks a path up and down my neck.

"Yessss," Dax hisses. "God, I've missed you."

"I know." It's all I can say as he drives me closer and closer to release. He reaches between us, strumming my clit. "Dax!"

I don't care how loud I am as I come. Stars burst behind my eyes as my orgasm washes over me. It only takes a few more thrusts before I feel Dax emptying into the condom.

"So fucking good, Sunshine. So good."

"Perfect."

Everything about this moment is perfect.

The two of us together. Forging our own life together without the worry of anyone else. It's everything I could have ever wanted.

Someone to love me for me. Who supports me and my crazy dreams.

"I love you, Chloe," Dax whispers into my neck.

"I love you too."

It's all that needs to be said. Because as long as the two of us are together, we'll be okay.

I know it.

Epilogue

CHLOE - THREE YEARS LATER

I don't think this morning could get any better.

A cup of tea by the pool. The sun high in the sky. Floating in the cool water. Only one thing could make this better.

"Morning, Sunshine."

And there he is.

Flipping over, I see Dax pulling his shirt off and toeing out of his tennis shoes. In the full light of the midmorning sun, he looks as sexy as ever.

"Hey, husband."

Stripping out of the rest of his clothes, he dives into the water, slicing through it then popping up right next to me.

"I missed you." He drops a kiss on my shoulder.

"You didn't have to go for a run," I tell him. "You could have joined me for a morning dip."

He wraps his arms around my bare waist and pulls me close as I link my legs together over his ass.

"You know how hot it's going to get today," he fires back. "And now I have all day to do nothing but lie in the pool with you."

"Oh, yeah? That's all you want to do?"

I push my bare chest against his, loving the heat that flares through my body.

Dax kisses just below my ear. "I think a hike down to the beach might be nice too."

"A hike? Really?"

This time, a kiss to my jaw. His hands roam down, squeezing my ass and pulling me into his hardening cock.

"Working up a sweat with you? Definitely."

"I could think of a much more enjoyable way to work up a sweat besides that."

"What'd you have in mind, wifey?"

I smile at him. There is nothing I love hearing more than Dax calling me *wifey*.

"Oh, I don't know. Maybe something along the lines of working up a sweat in the bedroom." I waggle my eyebrows.

Dax turns, resting my back against the wall of the infinity pool. Even from the cliff our private villa rests on, the sounds of the waves echo around us.

"You mean the two orgasms I gave you very early this morning weren't enough to satisfy you?"

Cupping his cheeks, I steer his dark brown eyes to mine. "I will never be satisfied. I will always want more with you, Dax. Always."

Dax seals his mouth over mine. I need his kiss as much as I need to breathe. Heat floods through my veins as I dig my fingers into his back. The cold metal of the chain he wears presses into my skin as his tongue slides along mine.

I welcome him in, sucking on his tongue. His hands roam down my sides, tweaking my already hard nipples. Everything about Dax turns me on.

He trails his lips down across my jaw. Nibbling and sucking on the tender skin below my ear.

"Will you accept the pool, Sunshine?"

I reach between us and squeeze his cock in response. "Yes. I need you, Dax."

"God, I love you." Dax pulls back and lines himself up before thrusting into me.

"Yes!" I shout.

Our kisses are slow and lazy as Dax moves in and out of me. In the warm water, it's perfect. I dig my heels into his ass to urge him on the closer I get to release.

I'm greedy for my husband. I'll never get over the feeling of him stretching me and filling me like this.

"I'm so close, Dax. Please."

He speeds up without a word, moving his hand between the two of us to play with my clit like he knows I love.

"Are you going to come, Chloe? I'm close," he growls.

Digging my nails into his back, I hold on as I tip over the edge into pure heaven.

"Gah!"

His moves falter, pick up, and in a few more thrusts, he's coming inside me. If it weren't for Dax holding me right now, I'd float away.

"Oh Dax."

"So good, Sunshine." He presses warm kisses up my neck. "You know, I really could get used to this."

"Sex in the pool?" I ask.

"That. Skinny-dipping. You might have been onto something."

"Well, if we get to take more trips like this after the season, I could get used to it too."

Dax spins my lax body in the pool, trailing his fingers over my stomach. "Well, hopefully we can do it again next season."

"Is that the only way we'll get to come back?"

"Technically this is a delayed honeymoon."

Sitting up, I push my wet hair out of my face and stand on my tiptoes in front of Dax. "Delayed honeymoon or not, I say we make this a new tradition."

He smiles down at me, cheeks pink. "After we win, or after every season?"

I drape my arms over his shoulders. "Every season. We can celebrate if you win, but it'll be a good way to escape if you don't."

"Breaking away from the real world, if you will?" Dax waggles his eyebrows at me.

"The store can manage without me for a little while."

"Good. The world's best boss can take a few days off."

"You're biased," I say.

"Not biased." He pecks my nose. "You didn't get that award for being one of the top workplaces in Nashville for no reason."

The Knights' playoff run was only one of the reasons we delayed our honeymoon after getting married over the All-Star break. Things with Charms by Chloe have been going better than I ever imagined. There were some hard months when we first started, trying to make a name for myself. But when Genevieve—still my favorite pop star—posted about it on social media, things blew up and I've never looked back.

I've been able to hire more staff. Bring in up-and-coming designers to sell their work. Give them the helping hand that I never got.

"I couldn't have done it without you."

"Nah. You did it all on your own."

"Did you think we'd ever get here?" I ask, playing with the wet strands of hair at the nape of his neck.

He shakes his head. "I hoped like hell we would, but I never thought we'd be right here."

"I didn't either."

"I mean, I'm not complaining." He smiles at me. "It's more than I ever could have asked for."

I grin back at him.

"Ditto."

Keep reading for a bonus scene with Dax and Chloe…

Bonus Scene

DAX - SIX MONTHS BEFORE THE EPILOGUE

BODE

You sure you know what you're doing?

NOAH

Would you quit asking him that? You're
going to make him nervous

DAX

I'm not nervous

BODE

You sure?

MARCUS

Bode!

BODE

Hey, we need to make sure he's ready

I'm ready

Dick

BODE

Hey, Chloe is the one that said she never
wanted to get married

GRAHAM

Do you know what you're going to say?

Did you guys do this when Bode proposed?

NOAH

No, because the fucker didn't tell us until after

BODE

Because I knew Stevie would say yes

MARCUS

Just like Chloe is going to say yes

Thank you!

I'm not worried

JASPER

She's going to say yes

MARCUS

Thanks for jumping in

BODE

He's too busy on the farm

JASPER

GRAHAM

Maybe we should get a farm

GRAHAM

That sounds nice

NOAH

Do you know the first thing about living on a farm?

GRAHAM

Jasper can teach us

NOAH

Jasper, do YOU know the first thing about living on a farm?

JASPER

I'm learning

NOAH

I rest my case

And now I'm going

MARCUS

Don't worry. She'll say yes

BODE

We're sure of it

NOAH

Oh, now you're sure of it 🙄

BODE

I was always sure. Just had to make sure Dax was

NOAH

Remind me not to tell you fuckers when I propose

GRAHAM

Why do you get to propose? What if I want to?

NOAH

Are you going to?

GRAHAM

Maybe I will

GRAHAM

Just to beat you to the punch

Seriously, leaving now

NOAH

You love us

I don't know why

MARCUS

Good luck, Dax. Go get your girl

BODE

Technically he already has her

MARCUS

Go bother Stevie, Bode.

BODE

I laugh, shoving my phone into my pocket.

If there is one thing I'm *sure* of today, it's proposing to Chloe. It's been almost three years that we've been together. Three of the best years of my life. I've hit every professional goal I've ever had for myself and it still pales in comparison to loving her.

We've talked about getting married. It took Chloe some time to come around to the idea. No matter how much she believes in our love, she's still scarred from that first time.

Well, almost first time.

When I broached the subject a few months ago, she was open to it. A small ceremony. Us and the guys. Our families still haven't come around, but that's okay.

We have our chosen family that loves and supports us.

The best part? I know exactly the kind of ring she wants. And pulled off some stealth methods to make it happen.

Checking the dinner in the oven one last time, I make myself a drink to help settle the nerves before Chloe gets home. I sent her out with the girls today. They're in on it, so they're making sure it's all about her without cluing her in.

I don't want her to be any more nervous than I am. Not that I'm *nervous* nervous, but asking someone to marry you is still a big deal.

I've checked and rechecked every detail.

Nothing about tonight is over-the-top. Chloe wouldn't want anything like that. Dinner with just the two of us? That's all we both need.

The sound of a car door closing has me smoothing a hand down the front of my T-shirt. Again, nothing fancy because I don't want to give anything away.

"Dax?" Chloe walks in, shutting the door behind her as she pops into the kitchen. "Hi."

"Hey. How was your day?"

Before I can pull her in for a hug, she stops me with a hand to the chest. "What's going on?"

"What do you mean?"

She peers behind me. "You're cooking dinner. There's flowers on the table. Something is up."

"Can't I spoil you?"

This time, Chloe crosses her arms. "What is it?"

"I really can't surprise you, can I?"

"Spill, Dax."

Grabbing her hand, I pull her farther into the house. It's then she spots the ring box sitting next to the flowers. I don't let her say anything before I drop to one knee.

"I know we've talked a lot about this, Chloe, but…" I have to stop and shake my hand out. I guess I'm more nervous than I thought.

"We have." She smiles down at me.

"I love you. More than I'll ever be able to express to you. I have never felt more myself than when I'm with you. You support me in ways I never thought I would ever feel. You're the reason I wake up every morning with a smile and the reason I go to bed happy. If everything disappeared tomorrow, as long as I have you, I'll have everything I need."

As I pop open the box, Chloe's jaw drops. A round diamond sits in the center of a yellow gold band, designed to resemble vines. One vine seems to loop around the diamond, then branch off to one side with smaller emeralds embedded. It's everything she wanted. Unique. Nothing overly flashy. Something that she can wear everyday while working.

"Chloe, will you marry me?"

"Wait. Dax…" Chloe fingers the ring. "I made this."

I smile up at her. "You always said you wanted to design our rings."

"But how in the world did you pull this off?"

"I had one of the interns on the team help."

Chloe drops to her knees, wrapping her arms around me. "I can't believe you did this. I told you I was designing something like this for a customer and it was you all along?"

I nod, pressing my lips to her neck as she admires the ring. "And you never suspected a thing."

"I can't believe this is mine."

"Well…"

"Well, what?" Laughter lights up her eyes.

"You haven't actually said yes."

Cupping my cheeks, she lays one on me. "If you think I will say anything but yes, you have lost the plot, Dax. Of course it's a yes!"

Tugging her close, I flip us around so she's on her back on the floor. "Hell yeah!"

I seal my mouth over hers, knowing that this is forever. That what we have will last.

Chloe pulls back, her face lit up with a smile, tears wetting her eyes. "Do I get my ring now?"

Popping it out of the box, I slide it over her finger. I already know it's going to fit. "Perfect."

"I can't believe you did this." She wiggles her fingers, the late afternoon sun catching the diamond. "I was creating my own ring and I didn't even know it."

"It didn't feel right to have someone else make it."

She shakes her head. "No. Not at all. But now I feel like I need to give you your money back."

I burst out laughing. "Use it for when you make the wedding bands."

"Deal."

Her eyes are focused on the ring, but I can tell her brain is already designing the bands. "You know there is plenty of time to worry about the bands."

"I don't want to wait."

"You don't?" That catches me by surprise.

"No. I know I want to spend forever with you, so why don't we just do it?"

"Okay."

"Really?"

"Ditto. To everything you said."

That has her laughing, pulling me in for another kiss.

"I love you, Dax. I don't want to wait. I'd do it today if it weren't a weekend."

"Next week. I'll figure out some time when we can get to city hall and make it official."

She smiles up at me. One full of love that matches mine.

I never thought I'd get this with her. To build a life together. One that we love. Just the two us. Doing all the boring things we could possibly imagine together.

"Good. Then why don't we take this upstairs and make it *official* official?"

Standing up, I sweep her into my arms and shut off the oven.

"I'll make this official all night, Sunshine. Forever, really."

"Just what I want. Forever."

JASPER'S BOOK, Bar Down, is coming October 24. Preorder now!

Author's Note

BOOK TWENTY-EIGHT IS OUT IN THE WORLD!!

Let me tell you…I was nervous with this one. I know we all love a dirty talking, growly hero, but Dax is the complete opposite. He is the ooiest, gooiest cinnamon roll hero I've ever written. He's soft and squishy, a walking green flag and putting him out into the world made me nervous. He might have put on a front in the other boys' books, but that's not him. He's down bad for Chloe and I just love it! He would do anything for her and I hope we all have someone like Dax in our lives.

Possibly my favorite part of the book? Duncan finally getting his due. He's the guy we all love to hate and to see him knocked down? YES! I. Am. Here. For. It.

I am going to keep the rest of this short and sweet. Thank you to all my author friends, Tina, readers, influencer team and everyone that has read my books. You are why I get to do what I love. It's been twenty-eight books, and here's to the next twenty-eight!

<3 Emily

Also by Emily Silver

Nashville Knights

Game Misconduct

The Playmaker

Breakaway

Bar Down

Colorado Black Diamonds Hockey

Best Kept Secret

Best Laid Plans

Best of the Best

Best of Both Worlds

For a complete list of all my books, please visit my website.

For a breakdown of my books by trope, check out my trope guide now.

About the Author

Image by Tricia B @TheSmutFairy

After winning a Young Author's Award in second grade, Emily Silver was destined to be a writer. She loves writing inclusive stories, with strong heroines and the swoony men who fall for them.

A lover of all things romance, Emily started writing books set in her favorite places around the world. As an avid traveler, she's been to all seven continents and sailed around the globe.

When she's not writing, Emily can be found sipping cocktails on her porch, reading all the romance she can get her hands on and planning her next big adventure!

Find her on social media to stay up to date on all her adventures and upcoming releases!